Nurse Alissa vs. the Zombies IX:

Calm Before the Storm

Nurse Alissa vs. the Zombies IX:

Calm Before the Storm

Scott M. Baker

Also by Scott M. Baker

Novellas
Nazi Ghouls From Space
Twilight of the Living Dead
This Is Why We Can't Have Nice Things During the Zombie Apocalypse
Dead Water

Anthologies
Cruise of the Living Dead and other Stories
Incident on Ironstone Lane and Other Horror Stories
Crossroads in the Dark V: Beyond the Borders
Rejected for Content
Roots of a Beating Heart
The Zombie Road Fan Fiction Collection
The Collector
Vlada: Tales of the Damned
Through the Aftermath: A Post-Apocalyptic Anthology

A Schattenseite Book

Nurse Alissa vs. the Zombies IX: Calm Before the Storm
by Scott M. Baker.
Copyright © 2023. All Rights Reserved.
Print Edition

ISBN-13: 978-1-7365915-9-8

Cover Art © Christian Bentulan

To Linda

Chapter One

DARKNESS FILLED THE void. The only light came from a dim sign on the far wall of the bunker, and even that limited illumination was dissipated by the dust hanging in the air. The smell of cordite permeated the area, the aftermath of the triple explosions that had collapsed the roof of the underground nuclear warhead storage facility and trapped Alissa and Chris in the reinforced cement tomb.

Alissa coughed herself awake. She crawled onto her hands and knees and hacked dust out of her lungs with such force that she lost her breath and gagged. Tears flowed from her eyes, and her temples throbbed from the exertion. Once her airways were finally clear, Alissa inhaled. This time when she coughed, the dust aggravated her throat, but at least she could breathe. She was lucky to have survived. Now all they had....

They.

"Chris?"

No answer.

"Chris!"

Silence.

Alissa felt around in the dark for him with no success. She unsteadily climbed to her feet, her head spinning momentarily when she stood, and cautiously made her way to where she remembered the exit was located. After two steps, Alissa tripped over a foot-square chunk of cement that had fallen from the ceiling. Her right knee landed on the jagged edge of a smaller piece. Pain shot up her leg. Alissa could tell from the wetness forming on her pants that she had torn the skin though, without lights, she could not determine the wound's severity. Her right arm bumped into Chris as she attempted to get back up. He lay amongst the debris on his side.

He groaned.

"Can you hear me?" she asked.

Chris did not respond. Alissa felt around until she touched his shoulder. She shook him.

"Wake up."

Nothing.

Alissa gently rolled Chris onto his back, careful not to drop him on a chunk of fractured ceiling. She ran her hands across his chest and face, searching for wounds. When her palm slid across his forehead, she felt blood.

A lot of blood.

Alissa slapped him lightly on the cheeks.

"Chris, it's me. Alissa."

He moaned and moved his head from side to side. That was a good sign. Alissa continued patting his cheeks.

"Talk to me."

When Chris did not answer, Alissa leaned over and kissed him long and lovingly.

"Hey, beautiful," he replied groggily. "At least I hope it's Alissa."

"Who else would be kissing you?"

"Slade?"

"Gross."

Chris attempted to sit up, grunted, and lay back down.

Alissa cupped his cheek in her hand. "Where does it hurt?"

"All over. I'm dizzy when I try to stand."

"Do you have a headache?"

"A bad one."

"You probably have a concussion. Let me help you."

Chris rolled onto his hands and knees. Alissa positioned herself behind him and placed both hands around his right arm. Standing was difficult. After a few seconds, and with Alissa's help, Chris made it to his feet. He teetered and would have fallen over if Alissa had not been propping him up.

"How do you feel?" she asked.

"Like a truck ran me over."

"How's your head?"

"Now that I'm up, it feels better."

"Lean back against the wall."

"Where is it?"

"Behind you." Alissa maneuvered him backward. "And be careful. The explosion left a lot of debris in here."

"That's right." Chris fell against the wall and groaned. "The bastard blew up the exit corridors and trapped us down here."

"We'll find a way out."

"You're optimistic."

"One of us has to be." Alissa said it teasingly. "There has to be an emergency exit. When you're ready, we'll look for it."

"Let's do it now. I hate the idea of being trapped underground."

Clutching Chris by his right arm, Alissa led him deeper into the facility. The farther in they went, the less debris they came across. By the time they reached the central corridor that ran the length of the bunker, the walkway was clear.

A sign that read EXIT glowed above a door at the end of the corridor off to their right.

"See." Alissa squeezed his arm tenderly. "I told you we'd find a way out."

"This is a secure facility. We'll probably need an access code to open it."

"Stop being an ass," snapped Alissa. Then, more gently, "I'll help you."

"Let me try it on my own."

Alissa released his arm but stayed close in case Chris stumbled. He took a few steps before becoming lightheaded again.

He fell to the side, coming to rest against the wall.

"Will you let me help you?"

"I'll be fine. I wish I had something to support me."

"Stay here."

Alissa returned to the debris field and felt around until she found what she wanted—a three-foot length of rebar with a small chunk of cement attached to one end. She brought it to Chris.

"Here. You can use this as a cane."

"Thanks."

The two made their way to the end of the corridor, Chris limping most of the distance. With every step Alissa took, the pain in her knee increased, and more blood oozed from the wound.

As Alissa had predicted, there was no pad to punch in an access code or swipe an identity card. She nudged Chris.

"What did I tell you? Piece of cake."

Chris leaned by the door and inhaled to catch his breath. The action made him wince. "You were right."

"You're definitely not feeling good."

"Why do you say that?"

Alissa placed her palm on the handle and pushed down. "You're not arguing with me."

She opened the door. Emergency lighting illuminated both the stairwell and a deader in camouflage BDUs that stood on the other side. Two more were on the stairs leading up, both wearing similar blood-soaked uniforms, the larger one missing an arm. The three spun around to face Alissa. The closest snarled and attacked.

Alissa slammed shut the door, catching the deader's hand between it and the frame. The thing pushed, shoving her back several inches. The BDU deader managed to get its head through the opening. Alissa slammed her weight against the door. The edge caught the deader in the right temple, driving its head against the jamb with a loud crack. It stopped moving.

Alissa moved back half a foot and slammed the door again. This time its skull ruptured, the bones caving in and exploding brain matter across the wall and Chris.

The other two reached the bottom of the stairs and shoved against the door, knocking Alissa off balance and forcing their way into the bunker.

The large deader missing its left arm spotted Chris and lunged, pushing him into the corner. Chris momentarily blacked out when his head hit the wall. He and the deader slid to the floor. Chris let go of the rebar and shoved both hands under its chin, holding it back. Pain pounded through Chris' head. His arms started to give way.

The deader's head pushed closer, the rotting teeth snapping inches from Chris' face. The stench of putrefaction filled his senses. A rotten tooth and bits of decayed flesh from a previous victim fell out of its mouth onto Chris. He gagged. Summoning all his energy, Chris tightened his elbows. The sudden movement caused his right hand to slide along the thing's neck and chin, peeling off the flesh. Chris quickly repositioned his right hand, driving the knuckles underneath the deader's jaw to hold it in place. With his left, he reached for the makeshift cane, his fingers wrapping around the rebar. Given his position and weakness, using it as a hammer would be impossible, so he went with the second option. Chris clutched the metal in his left hand and moved the rebar until the end rested against the deader's right temple. He slid his right hand along the opposite side of the deader's head and shoved, driving the metal deep into its skull. The body went limp and collapsed on top of him. Chris was too exhausted to push it off.

The second deader, half its face eaten off, went after Alissa. She retreated, putting as much distance as possible between them, then stopped. As it closed in, Alissa placed her right hand against her chest and swung her elbow into the deader's jaw. The blow knocked out several teeth and knocked it off balance. Alissa jumped back, turned at a ninety-degree angle to it, and kicked to the side with her right leg, shattering its kneecap. The deader fell onto the concrete, some of its facial bones cracking from the impact. The thing tried to crawl back to its feet, but she kicked out one of its arms, collapsing it onto the floor again.

Before it could try to stand a second time, Alissa raised her left leg and slammed her foot on the back of its skull. Another crack. The faceless deader's head deformed under the pressure, yet it still thrashed about. Alissa raised her leg and brought her foot down a second time. The skull collapsed. The skin on its right temple ruptured, spilling its brains onto the floor.

A sound from behind caught her attention. Another deader, also in BDUs, centered itself in the doorway. On spotting Alissa, it growled, the sound more horrific than normal due to decayed vocal cords. The thing stumbled toward her on a broken leg.

Alissa crouched and patted the faceless deader's hips, hoping to find a firearm. Her hand slid across the metal of a semiautomatic pistol. Unable to see well in the limited light, she felt around until she found the holster, unbuttoned the safety strap, and withdrew the weapon. By now, the deader had approached to within ten feet. She stood and rushed forward, using her left hand to grasp the deader by the neck, then placed the barrel against its forehead and fired a single round. From the light coming from the stairwell, Alissa saw the spray of blood and brain matter erupt from the back of the deader's head and watched it drop to the floor.

"Chris, are you okay?"

"I've been better." The grogginess in his voice confirmed that.

"Hang on. I'll be right over."

Alissa checked the deaders for sidearms. Two were unarmed. The one she had stolen the weapon from, a Sig Sauer M-17, carried two extra magazines on its belt. The one she killed in the stairwell also carried a Sig Sauer and two magazines. She slid both sidearms between her pants and her back and placed the magazines in her pockets. At least she had something to defend them with, which would be fine so long as they did not run into Slade's people or a horde of the living dead.

Alissa went over to Chris and helped him stand. When he was on his feet, he fell against the wall, clutched his head, and vomited.

"Do you think you can make it up the stairs?"

"I have no choice. Unless you want to carry me."

"No way."

She held open the door to the emergency escape and reached out for Chris. "Let me help you."

Chris brushed her off. "Thanks, but I can do it myself."

"You have a concussion. It's okay to ask for help."

"If I can't take care of myself, you'll have to leave me. I'm a liability."

Alissa knew he was right, even though she refused to admit it.

Getting out of the bunker took longer than expected. Alissa would move up to a landing, ensure no deaders were nearby, and signal for Chris. He would then climb the steps one at a time, slowly, using the guardrail as support. When he reached Alissa, she would wait a minute for him to catch his breath and move up to the next landing, repeating the process. The climbing did no good for Alissa's injured knee, the pain and bleeding increasing the farther up they went. After close to thirty minutes, the two reached the top of the stairwell. Another doorway stood in front of them. God only knows what they would find on the other side.

"Are you ready?" asked Alissa.

Chris leaned against the wall and closed his eyes. "Can I take a nap first?"

"No." She gently shook him. "You have a concussion. Sleep is the worst thing for you. Stay awake. I need you to open the door."

"I should be able to do that." Chris nearly stumbled over himself. He placed his hand on the handle. "Ready?"

"Just a second." Alissa withdrew both Sig Sauers from behind her back and aimed them in front of her, bracing for an attack. "Do it."

Chris turned the handle and pushed open the door.

The only thing that poured through the opening was a desert breeze and the last rays of a beautiful sunset. The western horizon glowed with a yellow hue that painted the bottom of the clouds in brilliant orange and red. The only sounds came from the wind. No gunfire. No humans. And, thankfully, no deaders.

Alissa stepped onto the sand and raised her arms to each side, pointing the Sig Sauers at her flanks as she searched for danger. Nothing.

Chris centered himself in the doorway, supporting himself against the frame. "You look like a female action hero from a 1990s movie."

"Thanks." At least he still had his sense of humor, bad as it was.

"Where are we?"

Alissa assessed the situation. "We're between the two entrance ramps leading to the underground bunker." She stepped out further and scanned the area, finally pointing behind the exit. "Over there is the maintenance shed. Maybe there's a vehicle we can use. Can you walk?"

"Barely."

Alissa slid the Sig Sauers behind her pants, wrapped Chris' arm around her neck and shoulder, and led him.

As they circled the mound of sand at the end of the ramp, barking broke the stillness of the night. Alissa withdrew one of the Sig Sauers, ready to take out any wild animals seeking food. Instead, Shithead raced up, his tongue hanging out of his mouth and his tail wagging furiously. He jumped up, almost knocking Chris over as he placed his front paws on his master's shoulders and licked his face. Alissa had all she could do to keep Chris propped up.

"It's good to see you, boy." Chris hugged the dog.

Having gotten attention from his master, Shithead moved over and gave Alissa a face bath.

Chris petted the dog. "What are you doing here, boy? Did they leave you?"

"He probably stayed behind to wait for you." Alissa motioned with her head. "Isn't that our car?"

Sure enough, their Challenger sat by the end of the ramp where they had left it. Alissa helped Chris toward it. Shithead ran around them, barking and jumping. When they got to the car, Chris let go of Alissa and steadied himself on the fender.

Chris patted the hood. "Now we have a way home."

Alissa hoped the car had been left by choice and not because their friends had been killed or captured.

Chris slowly made his way to the driver's side.

"What are you doing?"

"I'm going to drive us back to base."

"You can barely walk. There's no way I'm letting you behind the wheel."

Holding Chris' arm, she led him around the front of the car and helped him into the passenger seat. As Alissa fastened his seatbelt, Shithead jumped in the open driver's door, crawled in back, leaned forward, and licked his master's face. Alissa slid into the driver's seat, started the engine, and made a wide U-turn.

They drove by the maintenance shed where the battle between their people and Slade's had taken place. The ambulance, dump truck, and fire engine had been abandoned. Scores of deaders and pools of dissolved bodies melted by sulfuric acid sat amongst the vehicles. Alissa averted her eyes, not wanting to think of all those lost because of Slade's insanity and how her friends' remains had to be left behind in so undignified a manner. She headed for the main entrance.

Several living dead still roamed the compound, the few survivors of the slaughter. They shifted their attention to the Challenger as it passed and set off after them but were too far away to pose any danger.

Alissa exited the guard gate to Kirtland Air Force Base and passed by the terminal for Albuquerque Airport. The oil tanks in the center of the airfield still burned from being ignited by Slade, the flames lighting up the night sky. A few minutes later, Alissa exited onto the on-ramp to I-25 South and headed for White Sands.

"We should be home soon."

Chris said nothing. Alissa glanced over and saw he had fallen asleep. "You can't take a nap while you have a concussion."

No response.

She reached over with her right hand and tapped his leg. "Wake up."

Still no response.

Alissa turned to Chris and shook him hard. "Come on. You have to stay awake until we—"

Shithead barked and dove to the floor.

Alissa switched her attention forward. The rear end of a Mercedes Benz delivery van sat directly in front of them. She swerved to the right, missing it by inches, and slammed on the brakes. The Challenger slid several feet, bounced over the curb, and dropped down the embankment. Alissa's head banged against the side window, knocking her unconscious. The car continued down the embankment, rolled to the left until parallel with the highway, and sat idle.

FROM THEIR POSITION on the top of a nearby sand dune, Roni watched the Challenger wreck itself. "People drive like assholes even in the apocalypse."

"Should we help them?" asked O'Brien.

"I don't know if they're one of us or one of them."

"I thought we always helped those in need?"

"That changed when they started invading our territory."

The whining of a dog came from the Challenger. O'Brien looked at Roni and raised an eyebrow.

The woman sighed. "Now we have to help them. Keep your weapon ready. If anyone fires at us, blast the hell out of the car and everyone in it."

Roni and O'Brien stood and descended the sand dune.

Chapter Two

LINDSEY SAT ON the picnic table, her feet resting on the wooden seat. She had spent close to half an hour watching Abney tinker uselessly with the group's remaining vehicles. They had lost two during the battle with Slade's people at Kirtland. The only ones they now had were their RAM and the Humvee commandeered from the Scavengers. Abney examined the RAM closely, studying the damage and checking every detail as if he were a skinflint getting ready to finagle the asking price for a used car. However, whereas Abney usually spent his time in the motor pool constructively, using it to repair or modify their vehicles, now he merely wasted time. Lindsey knew the truth. Abney was not avoiding work.

He was avoiding visiting their friends at the infirmary.

The battle at the Kirtland Underground Munitions Maintenance Security Compound, otherwise known as the KUMMSC, had taken a heavy toll on the rest of the group. Brian had been killed during the first few minutes, having been doused with sulfuric acid. Alissa and Chris were presumed dead, trapped in the underground nuclear storage bunker when Slade blew it up. Thankfully, no one else in their group had been lost, although the injuries their friends sustained would more than likely sideline them from ever being desert runners again. The sulfuric acid spray from the fire engine had been as effective against their people as against the deaders. The acid had caused second- and third-degree burns on Fifty-Fifty's right arm, the right side of Liam's face, and both of

Tupoc's hands. Tupoc would never regain full function in his hands, and Fifty-Fifty would have to undergo months of treatment and therapy before he could use his right arm again. All three would be horribly scarred for life. When the ambulance was rammed, Malcolm suffered a broken left arm and leg as well as internal injuries. The infirmary had yet to determine the latter's extent or whether they were life-threatening.

The only ones not hurt in yesterday's confrontation were herself, Abney, and Kiera. Almost two-thirds of their group had been put out of commission in less than an hour. You did not have to be a military historian to realize a casualty rate that severe meant the desert runners would probably be disbanded.

Lindsey glanced at her watch. It read twelve minutes to nine.

"Honey."

Abney ignored her.

This time she called out louder. "Abney."

He looked up, though he was still clearly lost in his thoughts.

"Yeah?"

"It's time to go."

"Go where?"

Lindsey climbed down from the picnic table and crossed the yard. "We have the meeting with the president to brief her about yesterday."

"Do we have to go?"

"Yes. We're the only ones left who can talk about what happened." Lindsey's words sent a shiver through her soul.

"What's there to tell? Slade won. We lost."

Lindsey forced a smile. "I think she'll want more details than that."

"What good will it do?"

Lindsey wrapped her arms around Abney's right arm and gently led him away.

"Come on. Afterward, we'll go check on the guys."

13

PRESIDENT MARTINETTI STARED at the aerial photograph of White Sands on the wall across from her desk. Her gaze fixed on the image, but her mind was elsewhere. She still had not come to grips with their failure to prevent Slade from acquiring a nuclear warhead. The news reached her office early in the evening after the desert runners returned to base, having suffered incredibly heavy casualties. She had wanted to call an emergency meeting last night, but Abney and Lindsey were busy tending to their friends, Dr. Carrington was attempting to confirm the success of the curative formula for deader bites, and the military staff was determining the yield of the weapon or weapons stolen by Slade.

A knock sounded on the door to the outer office, snapping Martinetti back to reality. "Yes?"

Jill Sweeney, her chief of staff, opened the door and stuck her head into the new Oval Office. "Everyone is here. We're ready when you are."

"We might as well get this over with." Martinetti stood, straightened her outfit, and came around the front of the desk to greet the attendees.

The military personnel entered first. General Douglas Meyers led the way. He was followed by Colonel Ian Roberts, the officer responsible for base defense, and Major Sam Frank, who oversaw the military operations off camp that had warned them of the approach of Slade's forces. Cheri Martin accompanied them, the young woman from the Scavenger raiding party who had been detained while attempting to retrieve the vehicles left behind from a previous raid and who had been instrumental in helping them counter yesterday's raid on Alamogordo. Dr. Carrington and Nathan followed, both of whom had been working on developing and testing a cure to the deader virus; Martinetti prayed they had good news.

Bringing up the rear were Abney and Lindsey, among the few who had survived the fight at Kirtland unscathed. Jill entered last, closing the door behind her.

Martinetti greeted them with pleasantries and handshakes, then motioned for everyone to sit. She crossed behind her desk and, as she slid into her seat, forewent any more formalities.

"Let's cut to the chase. What happened at Kirtland?"

General Meyers looked at Abney and Lindsey, nodding his approval for them to begin the briefing. For a few moments, neither spoke.

"I'm waiting," urged Martinetti.

"Simple," answered Abney. "We failed to stop Slade and got our asses handed to us in the process."

The president bristled. "Are you serious? That's your brief—?"

"Excuse him, Madame President." Lindsey leaned forward in her chair, making eye contact with Martinetti while placing her hand on Abney's knee as a warning to shut up. "He didn't mean to be so blunt. We lost a lot of good people and haven't gotten any sleep since returning from White Sands."

"We didn't exactly have a day at the beach here," said Martinetti.

Lindsey waited for the ass-reaming she was certain she and Abney were about to get. Instead, the president relaxed her demeanor.

"Go on, and don't leave out anything."

Lindsey spent the next thirty-five minutes describing what had happened at the KUMMSC. How Slade's people had ignited an underground fuel storage tank to lure the deaders away from the base's interior. The ambush outside the entrance to the underground bunker and the Scavenger's use of sulfuric acid, which took out four of their number. Alissa and Chris going into the bunker to stop Slade, only to get captured. The Scavengers breaking through the desert runners' barricade and escaping. And finally, leaving behind Shithead and the

Challenger so that if Alissa and Chris survived by some miracle, they would have a way to get back to White Sands. Martinetti listened intently, her elbows resting on the arms of the chair, her hands clutched in front of her chest, her expression stoic. No one asked any questions, waiting for Lindsey to finish.

When done, Lindsey leaned back in her seat. She knew those present had a barrage of questions to throw at her, but they waited for the president.

Martinetti leaned forward, placing her arms on the desktop. "Your friends that were wounded, will they recover?"

Lindsey had not been expecting that question. "Those that suffered burns should be all right unless the wounds become infected, but they're going to be scarred for life. Tupoc will probably lose the use of his hands. Malcolm will have a long recovery, assuming his internal injuries are not life-threatening."

Martinetti turned to Jill. "Contact the head of the infirmary and let them know they're to do everything possible to get those people back on the road to recovery."

"Yes, ma'am."

"Thank you," Lindsey whispered.

"It's the least I can do. Now, are you certain Slade acquired a nuclear warhead?"

Lindsey nodded.

"We didn't scare them away," said Abney. "They fought us off until they abandoned the facility, destroying the bunker on their way out. I'd bet my life Slade's people got what they went for."

"We're all betting our lives on this. Is there any way to get in and inventory what's missing?"

Abney shook his head. "We tried once Slade's people left. We were hoping to rescue Alissa and Chris. The underground tunnel and entrances caved in. We can't dig through the rubble, at least not without heavy construction equipment.

Unless there's another entrance that we weren't aware of."

"Even if there were, it wouldn't do any good," said General Meyers. "We don't have an exact count of the number of warheads stored at the facility, so we couldn't verify if any were taken or how many."

"You also have to consider," added Colonel Roberts, "that if any of the warheads were damaged during the explosion, anyone who goes into the facility runs the risk of radiation poisoning."

"Fair enough." Martinetti thought for a few seconds. "General, what's the maximum number of warheads they could have stolen?"

Meyers focused his attention on Abney and Lindsey. "How many vehicles did you say left the facility?"

"Two. A Tahoe and a Mercedes van." Lindsey turned to Abney. "Isn't that right?"

Abney nodded.

"It's unlikely they could fit a warhead into the Tahoe. My money is they only used the van to transport personnel. Considering that the facility contained mostly W88 warheads, I estimate they could carry one, two at the most."

"And what is the yield of a W88?" asked Martinetti.

"Four hundred and seventy-five kilotons."

"How bad is that?" asked Nathan.

"If one of those warheads was detonated in this room, the blast radius would obliterate or heavily damage every building within a five-mile radius, or one hundred and eighty square miles. Everyone within a mile of the blast would be incinerated or killed instantly by the overpressure. They'd be the lucky ones. Anyone within a one-and-a-half-mile radius would die within a few weeks of radiation poisoning. Most of those between a one-and-a-half and five-mile radius would suffer third-degree burns and absorbed levels of radiation that more than likely will cause cancer within twenty years."

A somber silence descended over the meeting.

Martinetti took a deep breath. "How could they deliver the warhead?"

"Most warheads are delivered by ballistic missiles." Meyers did not seem concerned. "But I doubt that will happen. The nearest missile silos are around Warren Air Force Base in northern Colorado and southern Wyoming. Even if the Scavengers could gain access to a silo, they would never be able to launch a missile."

Jill frowned. "We never thought Slade would be able to steal a nuclear warhead."

"True." Meyers fixed his gaze on the chief of staff. His eyes were as cold as his tone. "But there's a huge difference between breaking into a secure bunker that's been isolated because of the apocalypse to steal a warhead and breaking into a missile silo, programming the missile to target White Sands, figuring out the launch codes, and launching it. That's assuming the silo still has a functioning power supply."

Jill sunk into her chair.

"Besides," added Roberts. "Missiles already have warheads mounted on them. If Slade planned on using one against us, there would be no need to steal it."

"How else could Slade deliver a nuke?" asked Martinetti.

"Aircraft would be the next logical delivery system." Meyers shifted in his chair to face Cheri. "Any idea how Slade intends to use the warhead?"

Cheri shook her head. "I've heard nothing about where and how he intends to use it. Not even rumors. Until yesterday, I didn't even know he wanted one."

"Do you know if he has aircraft at his disposal?"

"Not that I've heard of. Something like that would be next to impossible to keep secret."

"How about drones?" asked Martinetti asked Meyers.

"A warhead is too heavy to be carried by a drone." The general glanced over at Roberts. "The only way to deliver it would be by land."

"That would be their best option." Roberts paused as he considered the option. "But it wouldn't be easy. Trying to break through one of the gates would require a major assault. Even if they succeeded, we'd have enough warning to stop them. They could cut a hole in the fence and try to sneak onto the base, but that would mean having to cross the desert. It'll be tough for them to get the warhead to the center of the compound."

"They wouldn't have to set it off right here. Between the effects of the blast and the radiation, a detonation a mile out would be enough to render the compound inhabitable."

"Maybe Slade's not looking to set off the warhead." The opinion came from Major Frank. "Maybe he intends to use the plutonium to create a dirty bomb to contaminate White Sands."

Everyone turned to Cheri, who shrugged. "It's possible, but I never heard anything about it."

Meyers ended the discussion. "In either case, Slade has to figure out how to detonate the warhead or break it apart for the plutonium. I doubt he has the capability for either."

"Don't count him out," warned Cheri. "He has this whiz kid working for him named Zach. Zach got the solar panels working again at Vesta and returned our compound to working order. He's the one who came up with the remote-controlled bombs they wrap around the deaders' necks. If anyone can figure it out, it'll be him."

"What was the casualty rate here?" asked Martinetti.

"No one at White Sands was killed or seriously wounded."

"Thank God for that. Did we lose any tanks or armored vehicles?"

"No. However, the unit guarding the main gate used a lot of ammunition stopping the deader advance."

"Are we in danger of running out?"

"Not unless they launch two or three more attacks like that, Madame President."

"How many deaders were lured to the gate?"

"My men stopped counting around three thousand and were only half done." Roberts grimaced slightly. "I visited the battle site this morning. The road and shoulders are impassable for almost a mile. Vultures and crows have taken over the area, and the number of flies and wasps is mind-boggling. The killing field has become a sea of maggots in less than twenty-four hours. The stench is so bad the clean-up crews have to wear gas masks, and that still doesn't block out the smell."

"Maybe we should leave the deaders there. It might deter Slade from using that road again."

"We're not cleaning up the mess," said Meyers. "Several of Slade's people were killed during the battle. I ordered Roberts' men to scavenge the debris field for anything useful, like extra weapons, ammo, and anything of intelligence value."

Martinetti nodded. "Good thinking. What are we doing about being prepared for Slade's next move?"

Major Frank cleared his throat. "As of 0600 tomorrow, I'll be posting lookouts at the same locations we did before the attack. We'll rotate the teams out every forty-eight hours."

"Colonel Roberts," began the president, "can we increase the guards at the gates and set up roving patrols inside White Sands to stop Slade's people from getting in?"

"Of course, Madame President."

"Thank you." Martinetti thought about her next question, not wanting to know the answer. "Do we know how long before we can expect the next attack?"

Meyers looked to the other officers, who shrugged. He responded, "We have no idea. It could be in a few days or weeks. It could be tomorrow."

"Damn." Martinetti took a deep breath. "Is there anything else I should know about?"

Roberts and Frank shook their heads. Meyers responded, "No, Ma'am."

"Excellent." For once, Martinetti felt a surge of confidence.

She switched her attention to Carrington and Nathan. "I hope you have good news for me, doctor."

"We do." Carrington paused for dramatic effect. "We believe we've found a cure for the deader virus."

A burst of excitement went through the room.

"Do you mean a vaccine?" asked Jill.

"Unfortunately, no. However, we were able to isolate the elements in Nathan's blood that allowed him to fight off the deader virus, make a serum of it, and try it out. The patient selected for the experiment was bitten by a deader and immediately administered the antidote. It's been more than twenty-four hours and he shows no signs of reanimating."

"Who did you get to volunteer?" asked Martinetti.

Carrington hesitated to answer, so Nathan jumped in. "Badger."

Martinetti was confused again. "Who's Badger?"

"He's one of the Scavengers we took prisoner, along with Miss Martin, during the raid to get back the vehicles left behind during the ambush of our convoy."

Martinetti noticed that Cheri averted her gaze at the mention of Badger's name. "And he volunteered to do this?"

"Let's just say he had no choice. I wasn't about to risk anyone of value in case it didn't work."

"But it did work?"

"So far, yes."

Carrington jumped in. "We're producing more of the serum and manufacturing our own versions of EpiPens to administer it. Once they're ready, we'll start distributing them inside the compound, first to the military and those who have potential contact with deaders, then eventually to everyone."

"How long will that take?"

Carrington hesitated. "It's hard to say. We're limited in how much serum we can produce since Nathan is the only donor, and we have to round up the material to make more EpiPens."

"Do you need anything from me?" asked Martinetti.

"If there is, trust me, I won't hesitate to ask."

Martinetti took a moment to study those in the office. "Is there anything else?"

No one brought up anything new.

"Thank you all for attending. Keep me posted, and let me know if there's anything I can do to help." As everyone stood, Martinetti called out, "Jill, Abney, Lindsey, please stay behind."

The chief of staff waited until everyone else had left, then closed the office door and joined Martinetti and the others back at the desk. "What do you need?"

"I want the three of you to work on a contingency plan to evacuate White Sands and move to another location in case Slade uses the warhead against us."

"You don't trust Meyers and Roberts to protect the compound?" asked Abney.

"I trust them explicitly. But my old man was a Marine who served in Vietnam and the first Gulf War. He always told me that no battle plan survives first contact with the enemy. If anyone can stop Slade from using that nuke, Meyers and his command will do it. However, I always hope for the best but plan for the worst. If Slade succeeds in getting that weapon on the compound, it'll be too late to do anything about it. I want to have a plan in place to evacuate White Sands on short notice and move our people to a safe location in case this thing heads south. You three are the most capable of handling this. Jill, you're the best organizer on my staff. Abney and Lindsey, you know the desert better than anyone. Can I count on you?"

"Of course, Madame President," said Jill.

"We'll do our best," added Abney.

"You always have. Thanks."

Jill led Abney and Lindsey out of the office. When they left, Martinetti leaned against the chair back, closed her eyes, and massaged her temples. A part of her wanted to be on the front lines during the next attack, to hunt down Slade and personally shoot that motherfucker in the back of the head. Everyone at White Sands had gone through Hell to get here, literally. It had taken them months to establish the compound, stock it, and set up a defense perimeter to keep the residents safe. The people of White Sands had done the impossible. They had created a thriving society in the middle of an apocalypse and made the first steps toward taking back the world from the living dead. For the first time, these people had the possibility of a future that did not consist of being on the run and under a constant threat of being eaten alive or turned into one of the living dead.

Until Slade made his appearance. To his credit, he had also built up a viable community, However, whereas she wanted to rebuild the country as a democracy, Slade was intent on establishing his dominion over the southwest with himself as emperor. Yesterday was Slade's first attempt to take over White Sands and, as her old man would have said, he took a good situation and made it FUBAR.

Now all she could do was wait for the next BOHICA moment and pray they would come out on top.

Chapter Three

NATHAN SAT ACROSS the table from Izumi, the young woman the desert runners had taken prisoner during the confrontation at Kirtland. He estimated her age to be in the mid-twenties. From the way Izumi spoke, the woman was either raised in an educated middle-class home or had gone to college. Since she stood five-foot-six inches in height and had a small build, not what one would expect of a deader hunter, he assumed her intelligence was what got her placed in the field.

That and her demeanor. Despite being captured, Izumi did not seem rattled. He could see the fear in her eyes, although somewhat lessened by the fact she had not been mistreated. Outwardly, she remained defiant, having spent the last ten minutes refusing to answer any of his questions about the Scavengers, their compound, or their plans for the attack on White Sands. At least she was not being an asshole like Badger, which meant she could hopefully be reasoned with. Which gave him one last option.

After a few more questions, Izumi leaned back in her seat. "When are you going to realize this is a waste of your time? I'm not going to answer any of your questions."

"Aren't you afraid of what we might do to you if you don't talk?"

Izumi grinned. "You would have already done it by now."

"Which means you're more scared of what Slade will do to you if you talk."

The grin quickly faded. "Can we end this? I want to go

back to my cell and rest."

Time to play his Ace card. "You can go in a minute. I want you to meet one more person."

"Fine." The huff accompanying her response was a touch overdramatic.

Nathan stood, stepped over to the door to the interrogation room, and opened it. "Sergeant Rizzo, could you bring her in, please?"

Nathan returned to his chair as Rizzo brought in Cheri Martin, the Scavenger who had been captured several days ago.

Izumi sat upright. "Cheri?"

"It's me."

"I thought you were dead. Slade said you all died when the troops from White Sands ambushed you on patrol."

"That's bullshit. Slade sent us back here to retrieve the vehicles abandoned during his failed raid against the convoy from St. Louis. We were given a chance to surrender, but some decided to fight it out. Only Badger and I survived."

"That asshole is still alive?"

Cheri frowned and nodded. Izumi rolled her eyes.

Nathan tried not to laugh.

Izumi's expression changed from frustration to mistrust. "Are you helping these people?"

"They're helping us."

"You believe that crap?"

Cheri took the seat beside Izumi and faced her. "Let me ask you something. Are you handcuffed?"

"No."

"Did anyone here rape you? Abuse you? Threaten you?"

"No." Izumi's defiance faded.

"Same here. Now compare that with how we were treated when Slade's people captured us."

Izumi blanched.

"Exactly." Cheri leaned closer to her colleague. "Do you

know what Slade's people did in Alamogordo?"

Izumi shook her head.

"They rounded up several thousand deaders and directed them against us. Thankfully, we stopped them. Can you imagine what would have happened to the women and children here if they had succeeded?"

Izumi said nothing.

"Do you know why Slade raided the bunker at Kirtland?"

"He wanted a nuclear warhead as a deterrent against outsiders."

"Slade plans on using that warhead against the compound here at White Sands."

"Bullshit," said Izumi, though with little enthusiasm.

"You don't have to believe me. You'll find out soon enough. Did you know two team members who tried to stop you were buried alive inside the bunker when he blew it up?"

Izumi's eyes widened.

Nathan jumped in. "I don't blame you for not believing me. I wouldn't be in your situation."

Izumi stared at Nathan for a moment, then switched her attention to Cheri. "Did they make you fight your own people?"

"No. They used me only as an advisor. But I would die to defend this compound. They treat me well here. I have free reign of the facility."

"What about Badger?"

"We keep him confined," Nathan responded. "He's still being an asshole."

"Typical." Izumi seemed confused. "What will you do with me?"

"You'll have free reign of the compound," said Nathan. "All we ask is that you don't cause trouble and stay with Cheri."

"To keep an eye on me?"

"Until you prove you can be trusted." Nathan shifted his

attention to Cheri. "Take Izumi to the mess hall for a decent meal, then get her a hot shower and a change of clothes if she wants them. She'll stay in the quarters with you. Is that okay?"

Both women responded yes.

"Then you're free to go."

"Are you serious?"

"I am. Just don't make me regret this."

"I won't." Izumi paused. "Thank you."

Nathan offered her a smile. Cheri stood and led Izumi out.

Nathan waited until they departed before gathering his things and exiting the interrogation room. Izumi seemed like a decent person. With luck, she will come around and join the group soon enough.

MIRIAM RETURNED TO the infirmary from the mess hall carrying a thermos of hot coffee. Her second, and she was only four hours into her shift. She had never been a morning person before the apocalypse. Even being surrounded by millions of the living dead did nothing to increase her energy level before nine in the morning. Miriam knew she would be refilling the thermos for a third time on her next break.

As she entered the lobby, Andrea smiled from behind the front desk. "You have a visitor."

"Who?"

Andrea pointed to the row of seats against the opposite wall. Miriam glanced over. Little Stevie grinned and waved.

"Why aren't you in school?"

Little Stevie pushed himself out of the chair and stepped over to his mother. "I came here with Kiera."

"And why is she here?" When Stevie started to answer, Miriam raised her hands to stop him. "Don't bother. She's here to see Malcolm."

Stevie grinned and touched his finger to the tip of his nose.

SCOTT M. BAKER

"Come on. He's my patient. Let's go check on him."

The two headed down the corridor. Miriam asked, "Where's Thor?"

"Back in the dorm room being terrorized by Archer."

Miriam laughed. "That sounds like Archer."

A minute later, they reached the ward where Malcolm and the others were recovering. Kiera sat on the edge of Malcolm's bed holding his right hand. Miriam took it as a good sign the teenager was no longer in a medically induced coma, though he still appeared groggy from pain meds. Abney and Lindsey chatted with Fifty-Fifty, Tupoc, and Liam.

Miriam went over and hugged Kiera. As she did, she smiled at Malcolm. "I'm glad to see you're doing better."

"As good as can be expected under the circumstances." Malcolm used his good hand to gesture toward his broken limbs.

Kiera became excited. "The best news is his internal injuries are not serious."

"Really?"

Malcolm nodded. "I bruised my kidney, but there's no serious damage. It'll hurt for a while, and I'll be pissing blood for a few weeks. Thanks for asking, Mrs.... I'm sorry, but I never caught your last name."

Miriam clasped his hand and squeezed. "Call me Miriam. You're family now."

"God help you," muttered Little Stevie.

Lindsey chuckled.

"Don't laugh. You're family, too." Miriam went over to the other beds and checked the vital signs of her patients. "How are you doing?"

Liam huffed. "Other than dealing with the fact I'll be disfigured for life, I'm doing great."

Miriam understood his dilemma. Liam would need a lot of counseling to deal with what happened. Unfortunately, they had no one at White Sands who did that type of work.

28

Tupoc tried to lighten the mood. "You got it easy." He raised his bandaged hands. "I can't even eat or take a leak without having a nurse help me. And I don't want to get into doing number two."

"Isn't one of the nurses assisting you?" asked Miriam.

"Yeah, but it's a male nurse. It's embarrassing."

Miriam adopted an air of fake flirtation. "I can help you with that if you prefer."

Tupoc's face flushed. "Ah… thanks, but no. I'll deal with it."

"Good boy." She gently patted him on the cheeks. Tupoc turned even redder, if that was possible. Miriam turned to the others. "I hope I didn't interrupt anything."

"Not at all," said Lindsey. "We were telling everyone about our meeting with President Martinetti this morning."

"Do I want to know?"

Lindsey gave Miriam a condensed version of the meeting, concentrating on the president's request to have an emergency evac plan in place. The idea left Miriam with a cold feeling in her stomach. It was one thing to evacuate civilians at a moment's notice. Doing so with bedridden patients would be exceedingly more difficult. She would have to bring this up with hospital management and work out a plan.

After Lindsey finished, Abney jumped in. "One of her biggest concerns is stopping Slade if he tries a direct assault on White Sands. I wish we had more firepower."

"We do," said Malcolm.

"What do you mean?" asked Lindsey.

"When we were at Kirtland, I noticed a pair of A-10 Warthogs sitting on the flight line."

"Nice thought," said Lindsey. "But I doubt they're still operable."

"And even if they were," added Abney, "I doubt any aviation fuel is still viable. Plus, we don't have pilots to fly them."

Malcolm waved his good hand to stop the discussion.

"You're missing my point. The A-10's primary weapon is a seven-barrel, 30mm gatling gun with over a thousand rounds of ammunition."

"So?" asked Kiera.

"So, we tow the planes back here, remove them from the A-10s, mount them on trucks, and we have ourselves a highly effective weapon to take on Slade when he attacks."

Chapter Four

S LADE WOKE UP from a sound sleep, feeling more rested and exhilarated than he had in six months. He reached over, pulled his watch off the end table, and glanced at the face. 8:58. He had not slept this late in a long time. Considering the stress he had been under the past few weeks, it did not surprise him. And the fact that last night he had celebrated yesterday's victory by screwing the hell out of Gina. A part of him wanted to stay in bed and relax a while longer, but there were too many things to attend to. He could relax later.

Swinging his legs out of bed, Slade stood, favoring his good leg. He slid on a pair of pants, socks, and boots and was putting on his shirt when a knock sounded on the door.

"Who is it?"

"Candolini," called out his second in command.

"Come in."

Candolini entered, pausing when he noticed Gina's naked body in bed, only partially covered. "Sorry. I'll come back later."

"It's okay." Slade motioned for him to enter. "What's up?"

"I wanted to update you on losses from yesterday."

"Bad?"

Candolini shook his head. "Not as bad as originally anticipated. We only lost twenty-one people in Alamogordo. The operation in Kirtland cost us six team members."

"If any of the casualties have family members, make sure they're taken care of."

"I will. Also, we lost nine vehicles, including the fire engine."

"It's a shame about that, especially after all the effort we went through to get it." Slade finished buttoning his shirt and stuffed the ends into his pants. "But we wouldn't have used it again."

"We should try and commandeer more vehicles before we attack White Sands."

"Agreed." Slade finished dressing. "I assume we used all our suicide deaders?"

Candolini nodded.

"We need to replenish."

"I'll send out the Pit crew to find some more."

"This time, I want runners. A hundred of them."

"That's not going to be easy," Candolini scratched his chin. "All the deaders out there are shamblers."

"What about those newly turned at NORAD?"

"The team gathered most of those, though there might be a few stragglers. But way short of one hundred. Even those won't be as quick as you want. They turned weeks ago. We'll need to find people who we can infect and reanimate."

"How many on the compound are expendable?"

Candolini thought for a moment. "Well, we have nine people in solitary for serious crimes."

"What about Big Jake's back room?"

"I think there's twelve working there."

"Pull them out and infect them."

"What about the men? If there's no one to satisfy them, we might have issues in the compound."

"It'll only be temporary. Once we take White Sands, we can refill the back room."

"That will still leave us eighty short," said Candolini. "Do you want me to take them from our compound?"

"No one here would ever trust us again. We'll have to find another option."

Candolini flashed his boss a conspiratorial grin. "We have contingency plans in place."

"Then do it. I trust you. And keep me posted."

"Of course."

Slade walked past his second in command and headed for the door. "I'm going to check on the status of our warhead."

ZACH SAT BEHIND his workbench, staring at the W88 placed base down on the floor of his lab. Two days ago, he was excited about the prospect of obtaining the nuclear device from the bunker. Yesterday he was euphoric because his plan to acquire it went off without a hitch, from blowing up the underground fuel tanks beneath the airfield to lure the deaders away from the main target to the actual operation to break into the bunker and remove the warhead. The raiding party had suffered fewer casualties than he had anticipated, and most of those resulted in the unexpected encounter with the party from White Sands.

All that evaporated overnight for two reasons.

First, Zach now had a nuclear warhead sitting in his work area. Despite all the prior research on the technical aspects of such weapons, once he removed the panel and gained access to the firing mechanism, Zach realized he was in way over his head. Dealing with the innards of a nuclear warhead was a far cry from repairing solar panels or getting water pumps back online. Taking on this task gave him two options, the only acceptable one being success in programming the warhead to be detonated at his command. The second option, and his biggest fear, involved fucking this up and either contaminating Vesta with radiation or, worst case, accidentally detonating it. The only positive aspect of those outcomes would be his instantaneous death.

Which led Zach to the second reason his enthusiasm for this project had waned. Until last night, he had always considered himself a vital team member, Slade's right-hand man, someone instrumental in the running of the compound. Slade shattered that fantasy when he dressed down Zach for not wanting to bury that young man and woman from the opposing side alive, telling Zach he ran the technical aspects of the operation and nothing else. At that moment, Zach realized he was not a key player but merely one of Slade's pawns, a chess piece to do the king's bidding for control of the game board. In this case, the game board was the southwest United States, and the only way for Slade to win would be to annihilate the other side in a nuclear holocaust. A nuclear holocaust he would create.

Zach had never contemplated the end game of his actions. He had come up with the idea to procure a nuclear device as a deterrent to keep Vesta safe from outsiders. He never intended to use it aggressively.

How could he have been so fucking stupid?

For a few minutes, Zach considered placing the barrel of his revolver against the roof of his mouth and pulling the trigger. Going straight to Hell would be a better option than killing tens of thousands of innocent people or suffering what Slade would put him through if he failed. He had nothing to live for.

That thought evaporated when he felt the warm, gentle hand of Tara slide across his shoulder. Slade had assigned her to Zach as his personal whore to keep him happy and, more than likely, spy on him. He refused to treat her like a common lay, but knew that if he sent her back, Slade would throw her into the backroom of Big Jake's, where she would be abused until she killed herself from despair or the Scavengers got tired of her. Tara wanted to be of assistance, so he let her help out around the lab. They became friends but did not have sex... at least until last night. And that was because they both needed each other. What had started as an act of kindness on his part had become mutual affection. That changed the dynamics of what Zach could do.

"Is that really an atomic bomb?" asked Tara.

"It's technically referred to as a nuclear warhead, but yes."

"Like the one we dropped on Hiroshima?"

Zach nodded. "Only this one is four hundred times more destructive."

"Jesus." Tara removed her hand and took a few steps back. "Is it safe to be in here?"

"No problem now. That might be a different story when I start screwing around with it."

"Does Slade expect you to make it functional so he can use it against White Sands?"

"Yeah." Zach's sigh gave away how he truly felt.

"You don't want to do this, do you?"

"No. What sucks is that I came up with this plan. Now I wish we failed at—"

The door to the lab opened. Slade limped in and made his way over to Zach and Tara, then patted the kid on the shoulder. "How is the conversion going?"

"I haven't started it yet. It's more complicated than I thought."

Slade's demeanor changed. "Are you saying it can't be done?"

"I can do it," Zach said defensively. "I'm just concerned that we could destroy our compound if there's an accident. Maybe we should move this project to another location."

"Any place we moved it would be isolated and vulnerable to an attack from White Sands or too close to deaders. We have to keep the warhead here."

"Do you think Martinetti might try and steal it?" Tara asked.

Slade glared at her. She stepped back and averted her gaze.

Zach cut off the argument. "If I were them, I'd try to steal or disable it, or detonate it here, rather than fight it out on their turf."

Slade thought about what they said. "You make a good point."

"Should I arrange to move the warhead off the compound?"

"No. We'd have to strip down our defenses to keep the warhead safe, and I'm not willing to risk that."

"What if White Sands launches an attack?"

"Don't worry about that. I'll bolster our defenses and set up a checkpoint farther south to warn us if anyone comes our way. You concentrate on configuring that warhead so I can detonate it. How long will that take?"

"I'm not sure. It's more difficult than—"

"You mean we went through all this for nothing?"

"No. But the process is more complicated than I thought. The detonation parameters are programmed into the warhead via computer. I need to figure out a way around that."

"You have one week to get it done." The menacing tone in Slade's voice did not go unnoticed, nor did the concluding threat. "Don't disappoint me."

"Yes, sir." Zach almost stammered his response.

Slade turned for the door, then stopped. "How many neck bombs do we have for the deaders?"

"Around fifty, maybe a little less."

"I need a hundred to arm the runners we'll be bringing in later this week."

"That'll be difficult."

Slade was not happy with the answer. "Is there a problem?"

"I can't make them and figure out how to detonate the warhead at the same time."

"I can help make them," Tara interrupted.

Slade studied her. "You know how?"

"Yes," Tara lied, hoping she was not getting her and Zach into deeper trouble. "I learned while watching Zach."

Slade smiled. "Then it's settled. Zach, you figure out how

to detonate the warhead and Tara will build the neck bombs. Keep me informed of the progress."

Zach waited a few seconds after Slade left before asking, "When did you learn how to make neck bombs?"

"I didn't."

"Jesus, you lied to the Boss."

"I saved your ass." Tara stepped up to Zach and kissed him. "If I were you, I'd teach me how to make them, otherwise we only have a week to live."

MONICA SAWYER FOLLOWED the rest of her team into the Pit, the warehouse on the outskirts of the compound where the deaders were fitted with explosive collars. The job sucked on so many levels. Having to deal with the living dead meant dealing with the stench of decayed flesh as well as flies and wasps, though lately, their boss Vince had allowed them to spray the bodies with insecticide to diminish the aggravation. Dealing with the odor was a minor inconvenience compared to the dangers of handling scores of deaders. If the team was not out herding them onto the truck for transport back to base, they were removing the living dead from the arrival pen, wrapping explosive devices around their necks, and transferring them to the holding pen. It was the most dangerous job on the compound. The only assignment worse than the Pit was being assigned to the back room at Big Jake's.

As much as Monica hated doing this, she considered herself fortunate to be alive. She had been captured by the Scavengers a few weeks ago when they ambushed the train she operated between St. Louis and White Sands. She was the only survivor of the ambush and, rather than execute her, Slade brought her back to camp and assigned her to the Pit. So long as Monica did as she was told and made no waves, with luck she might make it through this ordeal until she had a chance to escape.

During yesterday's operation in Alamogordo, the Pit crew accompanied the raiding party and rounded up close to one hundred deaders. Today they would unload them from the trailer into the arrival pen and begin arming them. Another hundred chances to experience an excruciating death.

When they entered the outer office, Vince sat with his feet propped on the desk, his head against the back of the chair and his eyes closed. The sound of his team entering stirred him from his slumber. Shaking his head, Vince slid his legs onto the floor and stood.

"What time is it?" he asked.

"A little after ten," Devon replied.

"Shit." Vince flashed a look of disapproval. "You're over an hour late."

"We had a long day yesterday," Renee said with a frustrated huff.

Vince flashed her a withering glare but quickly backed down. "Okay, okay. Point taken."

"Thanks." Devon tried to placate his boss. "We'll work late to get the deaders armed."

"No need for that." Vince waved his hand. "Candolini came by earlier. The boss wants us to round up some runners tomorrow."

"Runners?" Paul glanced at the other members of the team. "I didn't think there were any still out there."

Vince's expression changed, showing displeasure. It quickly switched back. "I'll explain it all later. For today, keep ten of the deaders you gathered and get rid of the rest."

"Are you fucking serious?" Terry blurted. "We almost got killed collecting those things, and now you want us to let them go?"

Vince blistered and was about to chew Terry a second asshole when Devon intervened. "Where do you want us to leave them?"

"I don't give a shit so long as they don't find their way back here. If they do, Slade will have all our asses. Devon, take Terry and Paul with you. Wayne will be here at eleven to drive the truck."

Devon nodded.

Terry nudged Eddie. "I guess that means we get the day off."

"Nice try, assholes." Vince grinned maliciously. "The rest of you can spend the day cleaning out the pens."

Eddie sighed. "Are you kidding?"

"When have I ever had a sense of humor?"

Eddie punched Terry in the shoulder. "Thanks, shithead."

Terry rubbed her arm. "Sorry."

Monica refused to complain. Cleaning up after the deaders would be a lot better than dealing with them.

CANDOLINI STOPPED IN front of the door to the radio room located on the second floor of the main building. It used to be central to their operations after Slade had established his community at Vesta. Many of the current residents were found via shortwave radio, people held up somewhere seeking help, help the Scavengers readily provided. Everyone rescued appreciated the effort and willingly assimilated into society. Just as important, though not publicly stated, was that Slade used the radio chatter to determine which groups posed a threat to Vesta and sent raiding parties to eliminate them.

All that came to an end three months ago. With few exceptions, every group within a two-hundred-mile radius had either been rescued, overrun by deaders, or taken out by the Scavengers. Slade kept the radios manned twenty-four hours a day on the off chance they picked up a broadcast of value to the group. Open-air messages were how they knew about the transfer of people from St. Louis to White Sands. However, the transfer of people and supplies ended several weeks ago following the

Scavenger attack on the train from St. Louis.

Candolini knocked, but no one responded. Not surprising. He knocked a second time and, when no one answered, entered.

Sparks, the radio operator, leaned back in his chair with his feet resting on the table, a pair of headphones draped over his ears, snoring. Not that Candolini blamed him. Sparks had the most boring assignment on the compound.

Stepping over to the chair, Candolini gently shook Sparks on the shoulder, startling the radio operator awake. Sparks pulled off his headphone and became alarmed on seeing it was Candolini that had disturbed him.

"Sorry. I didn't mean to—"

Candolini waved his hand. "Relax. I'm not checking up on you. I need your advice."

Sparks felt relieved. He sat upright. "What type of advice?"

"The Boss needs a fresh batch of humans to turn into runners. What's available out there?"

"How many does he need?"

"A hundred."

"The pickings are slim." Sparks stood and stepped over to a large map taped to the wall. "There's a group of about ninety people in a fortified compound a hundred miles southwest of us at the Fort Apache Reservation near Phoenix."

"Is that the survivalist group?"

Sparks nodded. "Those guys are heavily armed and looking for a fight. I'd avoid them unless absolutely necessary."

"Agreed. What else?"

"There's the rogue National Guard unit outside of Vegas. About two dozen soldiers and forty or so civilians."

"I forgot about them. What's their status?"

"Not sure. They went silent two months ago."

Candolini raised an eyebrow. "Overrun?"

"I don't think so. At least, they never broadcast anything indicating that. My guess is they went quiet and are monitoring the circuits like we are."

"What do we know about them?"

"Not much. They're held up in a National Guard barracks. I have no idea how secure their compound is. Considering they're Guard, I assume it's well protected. Based on their numbers, I figure they have at least six .50 caliber machine guns."

"How so?"

"Twenty-four guardsmen. Four to a Humvee. That's six Humvees, each with a machine gun. However, since they were mobilized because of the outbreak, there are probably a lot more weapons than that."

"Agreed." Candolini studied the map. "Anything else? If I come back with nothing, the Boss will have my ass in a sling."

"The only other site I can think of is this." Sparks pointed to a location in the Rocky Mountains west of Denver. "It's a group of religious fanatics that rode out the apocalypse in a religious retreat… camp… church… I don't know what to call it."

"Are they still active?"

Sparks snorted. "Every day at noon their leader, Reverend Moon, goes live for an hour to preach about how the outbreak is a modern version of the Rapture and their compound is a sanctuary where the righteous can wait in safety until they are called home."

"You gotta be fucking kidding."

"I'm not."

"How have they survived this long?"

"According to the reverend, their survival is because they have been graced by God. My guess is that the camp is isolated and not easily accessible. It's sheer dumb luck on their part that no one has taken them out by now."

"I think we found our target."

Chapter Five

A LISSA WOKE WITH a start. She relived swerving the Challenger to avoid crashing into the Mercedes Benz delivery van, bouncing over the curb, and careening down the embankment. She involuntarily winced at remembering her head banging against the side window. Alissa raised her left hand to see if the wound bled but could only move it a few inches. A pair of handcuffs secured her wrist to the bed railing.

A bed?

Memory gave way to reality. She was not in the driver's seat of the Challenger wrecked on the side of the road.

Where was she?

The bed was like those used in hospitals, with adjustable guardrails to prevent patients from falling out, only much older than the ones used at Mass General, dating back to the seventies. It contrasted with the rest of the room, which was clean with white walls, tiled floors, an array of cabinets that ran the length of one wall, and a marble-topped counter beneath it with a stainless-steel sink in the center. At first, Alissa thought she might be in a hospital room, except it was too smalll, and there were no outlets on the wall behind her for monitoring equipment.

Alissa examined herself. She wore the same clothes she had at Kirtland, although someone had washed her hands and, presumably, her face.

Chris! Shit, what happened to him?

Two doors offered access to the room. Her bed sat against

the closed one on the flat wall. The door by the cabinets sat open a few inches.

"Hello? Is anyone there?"

She heard a dog bark followed by paws thumping against the tiles as it raced down the hallway. Shithead burst into the room a moment later, shoving the door aside. He ran to the head of the bed, placed his front paws on the mattress, and leaned over to give his mistress a face bath. His tail wagged the entire time.

Alissa scratched behind his ears, thrilled to see Shithead was fine.

"I'm glad to see you, too."

"He was worried about you."

A middle-aged woman stood in the doorway. She was approximately five-and-a-half feet in height. Her body was lean, though hints of muscles showed beneath her sleeves and pants legs. Her face and hands had the weathered appearance of someone used to hard work. Blonde hair with streaks of grey hung past her shoulders. Piercing green eyes focused on Alissa through a practical pair of eyeglasses.

Behind her stood a man, a few inches taller than the woman and twice her size. His clothes hung loosely, indicating he had been heavier. The man was bald with a close-cropped, dark-colored beard tinged with grey. He wore Harry Potter-style glasses. Unlike the woman, his appearance was softer, implying he had worked indoors before the outbreak. He carried himself with a confidence Alissa had seen several times over the past few months, a confidence born of someone not prepared for the apocalypse but who had survived despite the odds.

"I'm glad to see you're awake." The woman smiled and extended her hand. "I'm Dr. Veronica Carter, but everyone calls me Roni."

"Alissa." She raised her hand to return the gesture but moved only a few inches. "Do you mind telling me why I'm cuffed to the bed?"

"A precautionary measure. I wasn't sure if you were one of Slade's people."

"You've dealt with him before?"

"Not personally, but I've heard from those who have. I try to avoid them. I'm pretty sure you're not one of them."

Roni glanced over at the man and nodded. He stepped over to the bed, used a key to remove the handcuffs, and slid them into his pocket. "I'm O'Brien."

"Thanks." Alissa rubbed her wrist and turned her attention back to Roni. "Why are you so certain I'm not one of Slade's people?"

"For one reason, you're polite. I assume a member of his gang would be threatening me to let him go. Plus, your dog." Roni stepped over and scratched behind his ears with her right hand. Shithead turned his head and licked her wrist. "He's a sweetheart. He adores you and the man we found with you. If he likes you, you're okay in my book."

"That's a risky way to judge someone."

"I trust an animal's instincts." Roni moved closer to the bed and removed a small flashlight from her pocket. "Please sit up so I can examine you again."

Alissa swung her legs out of bed. The room spun slightly. She clutched the mattress and closed her eyes until the sensation stopped. When Alissa opened them again, the room sat still.

"Dizzy?" asked Roni.

"A little."

The doctor used her fingers to push open the lids and examine each eye. "You hit your head on the driver's window when your car went off the road. You'll have a bruise on your forehead for a while, but I don't see any indication of brain trauma. Do you have a headache?"

"A slight one."

"How bad?"

"A three on a scale of one to ten."

"Do you remember your name and what you did before the outbreak?"

"I'm Alissa. I used to be a nurse. My friend is Chris." She pointed to the German Shepard. "That's Shithead."

Roni seemed taken aback by the dog's name. "Really?"

"Well, his real name is Achilles, but everyone calls him Shithead."

"Why?"

"Wait until you get to know him."

As if on cue, the dog looked up at Roni and twisted his head, staring at her as if she was confirming Alissa's remark. Roni laughed.

"You mentioned Chris. Is he all right?"

"He will be once he gets some rest. I have him sedated in the room next to you. Would you like to see him?"

"Please."

"Can you walk?" asked Roni.

"I think so." Alissa took a few steps and, once confident she would not pass out or fall over, fell in behind Roni.

As they entered the corridor, Alissa asked, "Are you a physician?"

"A vet, actually. I did two years of pre-med and realized I couldn't deal with people, so I switched to veterinary school. You're in my clinic."

The two women entered the adjacent room while O'Brien stood in the corridor. Chris lay on a hospital bed identical to the one she had been on, only with an IV attached to his right arm.

"What are his injuries?"

"He has a mild concussion and a large bruise on the back of his head from where something heavy fell on him. I don't think there's any brain trauma or damage to the skull. It hurts when I touch his left arm, so I assume his humerus is fractured, but I can't be certain. I won't know for certain until he wakes up. I gave him a sedative so he could rest. Your friend was dehydrated, so I put him on a saline drip."

"Will he recover?"

"Of course, but it'll take some time. I'll know better once O'Brien gets the X-ray machine running again."

"You have an X-ray?"

"I have two. A small one for pets and a larger one for live-stock."

"What about our car?"

"The Challenger?" asked O'Brien. "It's banged up a bit. The front axle is bent, and the wheels are out of alignment. Nothing that can't be fixed."

"It's a shame we had to leave it behind."

"We towed it back. It's in the yard. I'm working on it now."

"O'Brien used to be a mechanic," Roni explained. "He's been a huge help in keeping this place running."

Roni motioned for Alissa to follow her back into the corri-dor. Before she did, Alissa moved over to the side of the bed and kissed Chris on the forehead, then joined Roni outside. Shithead curled up beside Chris' bed and took a nap.

Roni led the way to the opposite end of the building, with O'Brien bringing up the rear.

"I took the liberty of examining you while you were uncon-scious. Other than banging your head and being underweight, everything is fine. And your baby is healthy and developing well."

Alissa stopped short. O'Brien accidentally bumped into her.

"What do you mean 'your baby'?"

Roni paused and stared at Alissa. "The one you're carry-ing."

Alissa remained dumbfounded.

Roni tilted her head in confusion. "Inside of you."

Alissa tried to grasp what she had just heard.

Roni scrunched her eyelids. "You do realize you're preg-nant?"

"No."

Roni switched to a medical professional. "Have you been experiencing morning sickness?"

Alissa nodded.

"You've been hungrier than usual?"

"I haven't noticed."

"And your menstrual cycles have stopped?"

Alissa's eyes widened. "Are… are you serious?"

"I have an ultrasound machine in the other room to confirm it. But all the signs point to you being pregnant."

Alissa mumbled, "Oh my God."

O'Brien stepped to one side and stared at Alissa. "Are you sure you're a nurse?"

She turned to him, her expression a mixture of confusion and anger.

"Sorry." O'Brien took a step back.

"That's okay." She focused back on Roni. "I'm just… I had no idea."

"Not surprising." Roni continued down the corridor. "Our health is the last thing we're thinking of these days. Unless we get bit by one of those things."

"Your husband will be happy to hear the baby is doing well," said O'Brien.

"I'm not married." Alissa thought of Paul for a second and wondered what had happened to him.

"Either way, he'll be happy to know his child is okay."

Alissa hesitated. "I'm not sure Chris is the father."

O'Brien looked to Roni for guidance.

Alissa felt her cheeks turning red with embarrassment. "It's a long story."

Roni shrugged and kept walking. "Who am I to judge? All the rules went out the window when the dead started coming back to life."

"Thank you."

Roni stopped and turned to face Alissa. "I assume hearing

that you're pregnant is good news."

The woman asked a good question. Alissa was still trying to cope with reality and had not considered the implications. After a few seconds, she responded, "It's excellent news."

"That's a relief. For a minute, I was worried the baby might have been the result of a rape."

"That's the one nightmare I've avoided."

"You're luckier than most women I've encountered." Roni motioned for Alissa to follow. "First, let's get you a change of clothes, then I'll show you around the compound and introduce you to the other residents. What type of nurse were you?"

"I worked in the ER."

"Excellent" Roni glanced over her shoulder, a smile on her face. "You can assist me in performing some surgical procedures."

"I have no idea how to work on animals."

"You don't need to." Roni smiled. "I now run the local hospital."

Chapter Six

THEY EXITED THROUGH the back door into the parking lot. Everything outside the clinic appeared more like a farm than a medical center. A driveway branched off the lot and led to a three-story house a quarter of a mile up a shallow hill. To the right of the driveway, an area of two acres square sat enclosed within a wooden fence. A four-stall stable stood in one corner, the doors closed and no animals visible inside.

Five vehicles sat against the far end of the lot: a sixteen-foot Ryder truck, a thirteen-hundred-gallon bucket-style diesel tanker truck, a GMC Sierra heavy-duty pickup parked beside a towable car carrier, an ATV, and their Challenger. The front end sat on car ramps with chocks lodged behind the rear tires, allowing O'Brien safe access to the undercarriage.

As the two proceeded up the driveway, twenty chickens rushed from in front of the house to greet them, clucking and squawking. The flock swarmed around Roni, flapping their wings and looking up at her. A few broke away and surrounded Alissa. She bent down to pet them. The chickens lightly pecked at her palm.

"What do they want?"

Roni chuckled. "Breakfast. I was busy all morning keeping an eye on your friend and forgot to feed them."

The chickens followed them for a few yards, fussing the entire time. Once they realized they would not be fed, most wandered off searching for food. A small chicken kept pace behind them.

"We have company."

Roni glanced over her shoulder. "That's Fred, the baby of the group. He thinks I'm his mother."

"Are they being treated at the clinic?"

"No. They're mine. I'm self-sufficient. They provide eggs for me, O'Brien, and the patients."

"You're a survivalist?"

Roni grinned. "I prefer the term prepper."

"What's the difference?"

"When I think survivalist, I picture a bunch of people held up in a fortified compound ready for an invasion or a civil war and with enough weapons and ammunition to withstand a year-long siege. I wanted to be self-sustainable in case of an economic collapse or a natural disaster. Who ever thought I'd be preparing for an outbreak of the living dead?"

"How do you keep the electricity going?"

"Solar panels on the clinic and the main residence. I have backup generators for emergencies, though I've never used them." Roni pointed to a greenhouse beside the house. "I grow my own fruits and vegetables and can what I don't use. Rainwater is collected for washing and irrigating the greenhouse. There's also a water purification system behind the house for drinking."

"How long have you been here?"

"Nine years. I used to be a vet in Roswell but got tired of people, traffic, and noise, so I moved out here to the middle of nowhere. I picked up this clinic and house dirt cheap and converted it. I ran the clinic part-time for nearby farmers. I'd take care of their pets and livestock in return for their help setting up this place. One farmer sent me a hundred pounds of beef. It's stored in several freezers in the basement."

"That's a lot of food for two people."

"I have five patients here." Roni led the way up the steps to the porch.

"I didn't see any at the clinic."

"I only use that for surgery." Roni opened the door to the house. "This is the hospital."

Alissa stepped inside and paused, stunned by what she saw.

A large hallway ran through the center of the residence with a massive staircase off to one side leading to the second floor. Roni led Alissa into the room on the right. It used to be the dining room. The table had been pushed into one corner and the chairs stacked on top. A hospital bed sat in the center of the room with an elderly gentleman lying in it. An IV stand and a monitor stood at the end of the bed.

"This is Mr. Spritzer," said Roni.

The man opened his eyes and broke into a huge smile at the sound of his name. "Now my day is complete. Come give me a hug."

Roni went over to the bed and gave the man a long embrace. When done, the man focused his gaze on Alissa.

"I must have died and gone to heaven because I see an angel standing in front of me."

"Be careful of this one. He's a charmer." Roni gently rubbed his shoulder. "This is Alissa. She's going to be helping us out for a few days."

"Now I can die happy."

"You're not going to die." Roni checked the monitor. "How are you doing today?"

"As well as can be expected."

"Hang in there. O'Brien is making your breakfast now."

"What are we having?"

"Eggs and strawberries."

"No bacon?"

"We used it all up."

"That's right." He looked over at Alissa. "She's been very good to us."

Roni hugged Mr. Spritzer and headed for the door. "I'm going to check on the others, but I'll be back."

"Bring the pretty one with you."

As they exited, Alissa asked, "What's wrong with him?"

"A severe case of Type 1 diabetes. His right foot has started to become necrotic. I've been using maggots to eat the decayed flesh in the wound, but it won't heal."

They stepped across the hall and entered what used to be the living room. Again, all the furniture was stacked in one corner, and a hospital bed occupied the center. An elderly woman lay asleep under the covers.

"This is Emily Hobson. She has the onset of dementia."

The old lady sat up. "Is that you, Maggie?"

"Maggie is her daughter," Roni whispered. Then, loudly, "No, Mrs. Hobson. It's me. Roni."

"Is that Maggie behind you?"

"No, this is Alissa. She'll be staying here a few days."

"Is Maggie coming to visit?"

"I don't know yet. We'll see. How are you doing today?"

"I'll be much better when Maggie gets here."

"You take care. O'Brien is fixing breakfast. I'll be back to check on you later."

"Will Maggie be visiting me today?"

"Hopefully."

Roni and Alissa exited the room and headed down the hall.

"Where did they come from?"

Roni's demeanor suddenly became morose.

"O'Brien is the son of one of the local farmers. He worked part-time as a janitor in a nursing home in San Mateo. When the outbreak began, the staff abandoned the place and left eight people behind. O'Brien refused to let them die and called me asking for advice. I drove down in an old Ryder I have out back from when I was preparing this place. We loaded the truck with beds and medical supplies, then brought them here. Just in time, too. The town was overrun by deaders the next day."

"I thought you said there were only five patients here."

"Now there are." Roni swallowed hard. "Three have since

passed on."

"Sorry."

"Don't be. They died peacefully in their beds."

When they reached the top of the stairs, Roni pointed to the bedroom to the right. "Let me introduce you to the rest of our patients."

RONI SPENT THE next twenty minutes introducing Alissa to the last three patients: Fran Bishop, an eighty-five-year-old woman too arthritic to move on her own; Aretha Gibson, a seventy-three-year-old woman with a severe case of COPD; and Mr. Devlin, a feisty veteran of the Vietnam War who was mentally sharp and physically capable, admitting himself into the nursing home only because he did not want to live alone anymore.

They entered the kitchen as O'Brien finished preparing breakfast. He slid five plates into a tray delivery carrier to bring to the residents, then placed two plates of scrambled eggs and strawberries on the table for the ladies.

"Thanks."

"My pleasure." O'Brien picked up the carrier and headed for the door, pausing before leaving. "I made a fresh pot of coffee."

"You're a dear," said Roni.

Roni motioned for Alissa to sit before crossing over to the counter where the coffee pot sat. She took a mug off the tray and turned to Alissa. "Do you want a cup?"

"Yes, please."

Roni poured two cups, brought them back to the table, and placed one before Alissa.

"Let me know what you think."

Alissa took a sip. "Damn, that's good."

"O'Brien mixes two blends and adds a tablespoon of cinnamon."

"You ought to marry him."

"He's too young for me."

Alissa ate a few mouthfuls of scrambled eggs before asking, "Where are we?"

"You mean the clinic?"

Alissa nodded.

"We're on Prieta Mesa, thirty miles northwest of Albuquerque."

"How did Chris and I get here?"

"Luck." Roni took a swig of coffee. "O'Brien and I saw the smoke from where Slade exploded the fuel tanks and went to investigate. We were there when you crashed the Challenger. A good thing for you. I don't think Chris would have made it."

"Thank you."

"My pleasure."

"I'm curious. If we're out in the middle of the desert, where do you get the medication to treat your patients? Do you have a facility you raid to get medical supplies?"

"When we first took them in, O'Brien checked out every pharmacy and medical supply store within a hundred miles not swarmed by the dead. Most of it went bad when the electricity went down. It took several weeks to find a month's supply of insulin, so we had to improvise."

"How did you do that?"

"It's not easy. I extract a small amount of microscopic fungus from yeast, place it in a test tube, and spin it in a centrifuge to separate the proteins. Then I inject the protein mix into an electrically charged gel and, if all goes well, the insulin protein rises to the surface."

"And that works?"

"Not as good as insulin but, along with a proper diet, it keeps his diabetes under control." Roni sipped her coffee. "We've had to do that with all the medications."

"That's amazing."

"It's not as difficult as it sounds. There are a lot of home-made versions of popular drugs that are almost as effective as the pharmaceutical versions. You only have to know where to look. Thankfully, I had nine years to do the research." Roni ate a strawberry and washed it down with coffee. "The biggest problem is surgical procedures."

"Have you performed many?"

"None so far, thank God. But I will soon. Mr. Spritzer's foot needs to be amputated before the necrosis spreads any further."

"Do you have anesthesia to put him under?"

Roni nodded. "I have morphine for the pain and local anesthesia for minor procedures. The problem is the procedure itself. It's at least a two-person operation. O'Brien has no medical experience. That's why God saw fit to bring you to me."

Alissa did not like where this conversation was heading. "Why's that?"

"You're going to help me amputate Mr. Spritzer's leg."

Chapter Seven

MR. SPRITZER'S FACE lit up when Alissa and Roni entered his room. "My two favorite ladies have come to visit."

"We're your *only* two ladies," joked Roni.

"Even if I had a harem, you two would be my favorites. What can I do for you?"

"Alissa is a nurse and wants to see your right leg."

"It's pretty gross," he said with a touch of pride.

Alissa patted his shoulder. "I worked in the ER. I'm used to gross."

"Suit yourself."

Roni pulled aside the blanket and covers, exposing Mr. Spritzer's right leg. A stained bandage covered his foot and lower leg, stopping a few inches below the knee. Roni removed the twin hooks holding the end of the bandage in place and unwound it. The stench of decay invaded Alissa's senses. She had seen worse in the ER, but not by much.

The foot had gone necrotic. The great, second, and fifth toes remained, but the center two had rotted off. Decay had eaten away the skin around the missing toes and fifty percent of the muscles beneath, exposing portions of the phalanx bones, then continuing in a three-inch-wide strip past the ankle and halfway to the knee. Maggots crawled along the rotten tissue, debriding the wound. Several dropped out onto the mattress.

Roni pulled the blanket back over his leg.

Mr. Spritzer beamed. "I told you it was gross."

"I've seen worse."

"Really?"

Alissa nodded. "A guy in Boston riding a motorcycle and refusing to wear his helmet spun out on Storrow Drive. When they brought him into the ER, his entire lower jaw had been ripped away. The worst part, he was still conscious."

"Damn. He's got me beat."

"All right, enough of trying to outgross each other." Roni hugged Mr. Spritzer. "We'll be back to check on you later."

"Sure thing." His gaze focused on Alissa as he held out his arms for a hug.

Alissa obliged, embracing him from the side. "See you soon."

"I'm looking forward to it."

The two women exited the room and went out onto the front porch.

"How did his foot get so bad?" Alissa asked.

"Type 2 diabetes. It started at the nursing home. When I first examined him here, his toes and the lower portion of his foot were necrotic. I put him on a heavy regimen of antibiotics, but that only slowed the process."

"What about surgery?"

"I ran out of anesthesia a week before the outbreak. I never got my shipment once the shit hit the fan. If I wait much longer, the infection will kill him."

"Damn."

Roni hesitated. "There is a solution, but it's severe. There's a medical supply warehouse not far from here. O'Brien and I checked it out seven months ago. Few people know about it, so it hasn't been raided. The problem is, twenty deaders surround the building. I wanted to take the risk and break in, but O'Brien talked me out of it. He argued that if something happened to us, no one would be left to care for the patients."

"And you want me to accompany O'Brien there."

"If you think it's too risky, I understand. I have a bottle of Jim Beam in the kitchen. We'll get him drunk and perform the surgery."

Alissa spent a moment contemplating her options. "I'll go with O'Brien and check it out. Who knows what the situation is like now? If I think it's safe, we'll go in and get what's needed. If not, we'll come back and do the procedure with whiskey."

"Fair enough. Thank you." Roni took Alissa's right hand in hers and held it. "I'll have O'Brien reach out to you after supper so you can plan. The two of you can leave tomorrow morning."

"Okay. In the meantime, I want to check on Chris."

WHEN ALISSA ENTERED Chris' room, he lay in bed, sedated. Shithead lay on the floor beside him, looking up and wagging his tail when she entered. She grabbed a chair from the hall, moved it beside him, and sat. Placing her right hand on the bed, she interlocked her fingers with Chris's and gently squeezed. He squeezed back. Alissa leaned over and kissed his fingers.

She hated seeing him in this condition. It broke her heart. But at least they were alive, which was a miracle. The explosion in the underground bunker should have killed them. Whether because of fate or dumb luck, it did not. And Chris' injuries were not life-threatening. In a few days, a week at the most, they could make their way back to White Sands. In the meantime, she would assist Roni in getting caught up on her patients' health care.

A wave of nausea washed over Alissa. She looked around for a place to vomit, but the upset stomach subsided. Swallowing hard, she used the saliva to clear the bile in the back of her throat. Not that it mattered. The morning sickness would be back eventually, a constant reminder of the situation she had gotten herself into.

When Alissa said it that way, it sounded like she had made

a bad decision. Unlike some of the younger nurses she worked with who swore they would never have a baby, Alissa did not view being pregnant as ruining her life. She wanted a child when the right man came along, which was Chris. And when the time was right. Therein lay the problem. Who in their right mind would want to bring a life into this nightmarish world of the living dead? Her group had a difficult enough time as is surviving the past several months. Trying to do so with an infant in tow would only lessen their chances of making it through the apocalypse. The thought of her baby falling victim to the living dead terrified her.

Stop thinking that way, Alissa chastised herself. It was not like they were still on the road, threatened every day with being surrounded and overrun by deaders. Since arriving at White Sands, life had taken on some semblance of normalcy, or at least what counted for normalcy in today's new world. She only found herself in this situation because she had volunteered for this. Once back at the compound, she would retire from fieldwork and find a job on base. Chances were good the infirmary needed help. She could resume her career as a nurse and settle down with Chris, raising their kid like a normal fam—

A sudden realization suddenly struck Alissa. She could not be certain who the father was. Shortly before she and Chris had what they both thought would be their final fling in the lab at Mass General, she had seduced Nathan back at the cabin. She and Nathan had been friends since high school. What happened in New Hampshire was the result of unresolved sexual tension between them. She loved Nathan, but only as a friend. With Chris, that affection was genuine. Alissa could not remember when it happened but, at some point during this nightmare, she had fallen in love with him. It was the reason she did not mind dying with him in the underground bunker because they would have been together in the afterlife. For some reason, they had been spared. Though not religious, she did believe in fate and was convinced they had lived through the explosion to settle down, start a family, and maybe begin taking back the world from the living dead.

Fate or not, Alissa had made her decision. Once she and Chris returned to White Sands, she would give up being one of the desert runners and settle down.

Chapter Eight

THE CONVOY FROM White Sands was large since no one knew what they would encounter on the way to Kirtland: two flatbed tow trucks, three Bradley armored personnel carriers, four Humvees carrying sixteen soldiers, and Abney leading the way in his black Dodge RAM. Malcolm rode shotgun, clearly uncomfortable, especially when the pickup hit a pothole. Lindsey and Kiera sat in the back. They had been on the road since an hour before dawn.

The RAM ran over a desiccated corpse, bouncing the right front fender. Malcolm took a deep breath and grimaced.

"I don't like that we had to bring him along," Kiera whispered to Lindsey. "This is too much for him."

Malcolm leaned his back against the seat and turned toward the women. "I'm not going to lay around a hospital bed all day while you three go out and have fun."

Kiera became embarrassed. "You heard that?"

"My limbs are broken. Not my ears. Besides, I'm the only one who knows where the A-10s are."

"You could have told us."

"Do you know what an A-10 looks like?"

"No," Kiera reluctantly admitted.

Abney grinned. "I bet our military escorts could pick out an A-10."

"Whose side are you on?" asked Malcolm.

Kiera chuckled.

"I'm not on anyone's side." Abney swerved around a deader straggling down the highway. "I understand your frustration at being sidelined. And you're a vital member of the group. But I wouldn't have let you come along if I thought we'd run into trouble."

"Fair enough."

Everyone in the RAM stopped talking. After a few minutes, Lindsey leaned forward.

"Is that what I think it is?"

A pillar of black smoke bellowed skyward.

"It is," said Malcolm.

"But that was two days ago."

"It'll keep burning until the fuel inside the storage tanks is used up."

The convoy continued for another fifteen minutes until the outskirts of the air force base came into view. Everyone braced for an encounter with deaders. However, as the convoy drew closer to town, no living dead were in sight. The reason became apparent only when they neared the exit for Albuquerque International Airport.

Thousands of deaders lined the airport perimeter fence, reaching through and pushing against the chain links, their milky eyes focused on the tower of smoke belching from the center of the airfield. A few shamblers crossing the highway turned in the convoy's direction. Almost all of those against the fence ignored the approaching vehicles.

"One good thing about that fire," said Abney. "It'll keep them distracted."

The convoy reached the exit and took the off-ramp to the airport. A deader missing its right arm and left foot twisted at a ninety-degree angle staggered down the center of the road. Abney swerved to the left to go around it. The driver in the Bradley directly behind him slammed into the deader, the months-old body exploding like a squeezed ketchup packet.

They drove past the airport on their right. A few hundred deaders pushed against the terminal building and security fence. Abney raced past and proceeded to the entrance gate to Kirtland. The smashed Humvees from where Slade's people crashed through the roadblock still lay overturned. He maneuvered his way through the wreckage. The convoy slowed for a few seconds as the flatbeds decreased speed to pass through the gate, then sped up and followed Abney. A minute later, Abney turned right onto Pennsylvania Street SE. The airfield sat in front of them.

"There they are." Malcolm pointed with his good hand to two A-10s parked on the tarmac.

Abney drove over and stopped fifty feet from the aircraft. The two flatbeds pulled up alongside the aircraft. The Bradleys and Humvees circled them, the forty-six soldiers inside rushing out and forming a defense perimeter.

Abney climbed out of the driver's side and leaned back in. "Kiera, you stay here with Malcolm. Lindsey, you're with me."

Malcolm leaned over the center console, wincing at the pain. "Make sure they check that the guns on those planes are loaded. It'd be a shame to haul them all the way back to White Sands only to find they're unarmed."

Abney glared at him. "You could have warned us about that before we left."

"What good would it have done? There was no way to know their status until we got here."

"Fair enough."

Abney closed the door, then he and Lindsey walked over to the aircraft.

The flatbeds had already maneuvered into position to load the A-10s. The drivers lowered the ramps and unwound the hauling chains. As the first driver approached his aircraft, he paused to examine it.

Abney joined him. "What's wrong?"

"I'm not sure how to hook up the chain. I'm afraid I might damage it if I use the landing gear."

"Don't worry about that. These things will never fly again.

Once we get them back to base, the engineers will tear them apart for the weapon inside."

"Thanks, man. You made my job easier."

"My whiz kid suggests we check the guns first to make sure they're loaded."

"Smart idea, but no can do. The ladders we need to check them out are over at maintenance. We'll have to haul 'em back and hope for the best."

As the drivers loaded the A-10s, Abney took a moment to stare at where the underground explosion had occurred on the runway. Two days ago, an inferno raged at the location, attracting every deader in the area that flocked to the fire seeking food, willingly throwing themselves into the conflagration. The flames had shifted underground, leaving a mound of ashes and charred bones four yards in diameter and six feet high circling the opening. The sight left him with a feeling of defeat.

Turning around, Abney rejoined Lindsey, who stood with her back to him, staring deep into the compound where the KUMMC facility stood, and where they had lost Alissa and Chris in the fight against Slade's people. He stepped up beside Lindsey, wrapped his arm around the opposite shoulder, and drew her into him. They remained silent for several seconds.

"We should check on them," said Lindsey.

"We left them the Challenger. If they made it out, they would have returned to White Sands."

"What about Shithead?"

"Honey, face it. They're gone. Driving over there will only make you feel worse."

"But—"

Abney gently placed his index finger over her lips. "You know I'm right. We're inevitably going to lose people... our friends out here. That's just the way it is now."

"We've lost too many people these last few months. How long is this going to last?"

"I wish I knew." He leaned over and kissed her on the top of the head.

The whirring of engines caught their attention. Abney and Lindsey turned in time to see the two A-10s dragged up onto the trucks. Once in place, each driver raised the flatbed and secured the aircraft with chains.

A gunshot sounded behind them. A deader with its legs torn off below the knees crawled toward the salvage party. It must have come from deep inside the compound because the skin on its palms had been scraped away, revealing decayed muscles and bone. Bits of flesh lay scattered in the trail of congealed blood left by the thing. A Marine had put the deader out of its misery with a single round through the forehead.

The gunshot riled up the living dead lined up along the perimeter fence. Moans surrounded them as the mass of deaders grew frantic, desperate to get at the food inside. The straining of metal joined the chorus of living dead, followed by a metallic snap as a portion of the fence gave way. Scores of deaders fell through, creating a squirming pile of the dead. One by one, the deaders staggered to their feet and stumbled toward their prey, though still several hundred feet away.

"We're done," yelled the driver of the flatbed Abney had been talking to.

The commander of the ground forces called out to his unit, "Okay, people. Mount up and let's roll."

A minute later, once the soldiers had climbed aboard their respective vehicles, the convoy swung around, drove off the airfield, and was back on I-25 heading toward White Sands within a few minutes.

Chapter Nine

T HE CONVOY RACED along Route 40 on its way to Reverend Moon's compound. It consisted of the tractor-trailer, a
two-and-a-half-ton military transport, a Tahoe, and a Humvee
carrying thirty Scavengers led by Mauler. He switched his
attention between a map of the region and the written directions Sparks gave him. For all of Moon's religious pomposity
and Christian self-righteousness, the reverend never revealed
his exact location, placing his safety over that of those seeking
salvation and a haven from the living dead.

Sparks had determined the direction the broadcast came
from and marked it with a line drawn across the map. Of
course, that line stretched for several hundred miles. However,
from things the reverend had said, Sparks calculated the
compound was more than likely within a ten-mile radius of the
town of Granby, located thirty miles west of Boulder. Mauler
hoped the radio operator was right, or he would have to kick
some ass when he returned to Vesta.

Higgins, the driver, slowed to a halt.

"Why did you stop?" asked Mauler.

"Look at that." Higgins pointed to a dirt road on the left. A
series of tire tracks led down it.

"So?"

"They're relatively new."

Mauler checked the map. The road led to a resort in the
center of Williams Fork Lake. Mauler had to respect the
bastard. Reverend Moon had found himself a comfortable

compound with its own moat.

"I think we found the reverend." Mauler folded the maps and stuck them between the visor and the roof. "Let's go."

The convoy drove for three miles before arriving at the resort. The lake provided four hundred feet of protection between the mainland and the island. A luxury resort three stories high sat on the far end. A golf course stood in front of it, the grass long since baked brown. Several smaller structures dotted the shore, mostly maintenance buildings. On the left and right of the hotel stood a restaurant converted into a communal dining hall, and a gym that now served as the chapel with a large makeshift cross mounted on the roof. A two-lane road connected the mainland to the resort. Rather than being heavily fortified, a poorly-built chain-link fence with twin gates covered the road, a chain and padlock holding them closed, with a string of wooden sawhorses placed in front for additional protection. Thank God for naivety.

"Should we stop and open the gate?" asked Higgins.

"Fuck that," Mauler grunted. "I want to catch the mother-fuckers off guard."

Higgins accelerated and smashed the front of the Humvee into the barricade, shattering the twin sawhorses. Pieces of wood flew in every direction. Higgins aimed the right fender for the padlock, slamming open the right side and tearing the left off its hinges. Wayne followed a few yards behind in the tractor-trailer with the deuce-and-a-half and Tahoe bringing up the rear.

By the time the convoy reached the courtyard in front of the resort, a crowd had gathered around the central fountain. An older Korean gentleman, his black hair tinged with streaks of grey, black horned rim glasses resting on the tip of his nose, ran out in front of the Humvee and raised his hands, ordering the vehicles to stop. Mauler assumed this man was the reverend.

"What should I do?" asked Higgins.

"Stop, you asshole. And remember, Candolini wants us to convince these idiots to go with us, not force them."

Higgins slowed the Humvee and stopped twenty feet from Reverend Moon. The tractor-trailer veered right and moved to one side of the crowd. The deuce-and-a-half and Tahoe pulled up behind the Humvee and parked.

Mauler opened the door and stepped out.

Reverend Moon rushed over to him. "Who are you? What are you doing breaking onto our sacred ground?"

"I apologize." Mauler raised his hands in a gesture of kindness. "I wouldn't do this if it wasn't an emergency."

"What type of emergency warrants you violating our privacy?"

"How about a swarm of several thousand deaders heading this way?"

A panicked murmur rose from the congregation. Moon turned around and motioned for them to calm down. Silence descended over them, though they each glanced at one another in terror. Moon focused his attention back on Mauler.

"What do you mean?"

"Like I said, a swarm of several hundred deaders is heading this way."

"Originally, you said several thousand."

Mauler contained his anger. "What difference does it make?"

Moon turned back to his congregation and adopted his preaching voice. "As it says in Psalms 120:2, 'Save me, Lord, from lying lips and from deceitful tongues.'"

"Amen," they said in unison.

"Come on, man. A few hundred or a few thousand, what does it matter? You'll be overrun within an hour if you don't leave here now."

"We'd be safe from Satan's scourge if you had not violated our sanctity and torn down those gates."

"We don't have time for niceties," snapped Mauler. "Those

things are right behind us."

Moon spun around to face his congregation and raised his hands above him. "As said in 2 Kings 22:16, 'This saith The Lord, Behold, I'll bring evil upon the place, and upon the inhabitants thereof.'"

"Amen."

"I don't have time for this fucking shit."

Mauler removed the Baretta from its holster, placed the barrel against the back of Reverend Moon's head, and pulled the trigger. The round blasted away the front of his face and skull. A moment of stunned silence fell across the compound until a ten-year-old girl standing behind her mother cried. Then a mixture of fear and anger raced through the congregation. Several people screamed and ran for the resort. Some of the braver men moved to tackle Mauler. He swung the Baretta in their direction, stopping the attack.

At the sound of the gunshot, the rest of the Scavengers exited their vehicles and formed a semi-circle around the congregation, their weapons raised. A few rushed ahead, cutting off the fleeing church members and herding them back to the group. Higgins raised his AK-47 and fired seven rounds in the air, restoring order.

"Listen," said Mauler, attempting to sound sincere. "We need to get you out of here ASAP if you don't want to be attacked by the living dead."

"You murdered Reverend Moon," yelled a burly man with a red beard near the front of the crowd. His fists clenched so tight the knuckles showed white.

"I didn't mean to, but he was putting us all in danger."

"Bullshit," yelled an older woman from the back.

Mauler searched the crowd for a mother holding a young boy and girl close to her. "Do you want your kids to be bitten and become like those things?"

"No!" The woman held the children even closer.

"Then, please, come with us. If we were here to hurt you,

don't you think we would have done so by now?"

The woman's eyes kept shifting from the body of Reverend Moon to Mauler, uncertain of what to do.

Mauler decided to take a chance. He walked away and headed back to the Humvee. "None of these people want our help. Load up and let's get out of here before the deaders trap us."

"Wait." The woman with the two kids pushed her way through the others. "We'll go."

Mauler suppressed a grin. The one thing he could always count on was stupid people always making the wrong decision.

He glanced over his shoulder. "Wayne, get these three aboard the truck, and let's haul ass before—"

"I want to go," said a young woman with auburn hair who stepped forward.

"Me, too," added a middle-aged man who joined them.

The Scavengers shouldered their weapons, escorted those who volunteered to the tractor-trailer, and helped them in the back. Seven others joined them, running to make sure they were not left behind. One by one and in small groups, members of the congregation left the crowd and made their way onto the trailer. Within minutes, every member of the congregation had crawled aboard except three people, a woman who knelt beside the reverend's body and sobbed and two men who glared at Mauler furiously.

"Last chance," Mauler said to them.

"Fuck you," one of the men replied.

Mauler shrugged and returned to the Humvee. "How many do we have?"

"Sixty-three, according to Wayne." Higgins lowered his voice and motioned to the last three. "What about them? Should we force them to come along?"

Mauler shook his head. "If we do that, it'll upset the others. Leave them here and let the rest of these assholes think they had a choice. Three fewer runners won't change anything."

Both men climbed into the Humvee and waited. Once the congregation was loaded into the tractor-trailer, Wayne climbed into the cab and started the engine. Higgins turned around and headed off the island, the rest of the convoy falling in behind him. Five minutes later, they reached Route 40 and headed back to Vesta.

Chapter Ten

MIRIAM GOT OFF work late, having to stay an extra few hours to grade exams. Sometimes the difference between normality and the post-apocalyptic world seemed bizarre. Teaching was one of the few things she had left in her life. She had to abandon her home in Nahant and move to the safety of Alissa's cabin in New Hampshire, settling in there only to be relocated to White Sands when the U.S. military abandoned the east coast. Then, on the trip to New Mexico, her husband Steve had been killed only a few miles from the north gate during an ambush by Scavengers. Once Miriam had come to terms with what she had lost, including the love of her life for twenty-two years, she prayed for the strength to adapt to her new existence.

Even then, her faith was pushed to the limits. Kiera started dating Malcolm, and the two spent all their time together, which was not unusual for a teenage girl. What scared Miriam was that whenever the desert runners went out on one of their insane missions, Kiera accompanied Malcolm. Sure, Kiera had seen enough action since the outbreak to be a seasoned deader hunter, but that still did not prevent Miriam from being terrified every time Kiera left the compound. The last run to Albuquerque nearly proved fatal. Malcolm's left arm and leg were broken, though, miraculously, Kiera walked away unscratched. To make matters worse, Alissa, Chris, and Shithead were also killed in that raid.

Every time Miriam convinced herself others had lost more

and she still had her kids and a safe place to stay, reality slapped her in the face. No one at White Sands could ignore that they faced the threat of nuclear annihilation at the hands of Slade.

Even if the compound survived the next few weeks, which seemed unlikely, she would never get over the emotional and psychological trauma of the past nine months.

Miriam arrived at their quarters and entered. She hoped Kiera would be there but was not surprised to see her absent. Little Stevie and Connie sat in the middle of the room playing with Thor. Despite everything the poor girl had endured, she laughed and squealed in glee as the Labrador puppy jumped on her chest and nibbled her ear.

Archer curled up on Alissa's old bunk, creating a nest for himself from her blanket. On seeing Miriam, he meowed pathetically. How do you console a pet who has lost a loved one?

When the door closed behind her, Thor turned his attention to Miriam and bolted away from the kids, yipping as he raced across the room. Archer glared at him with disdain. Miriam crouched. When Thor reached her, she picked him up and hugged him, as much for her benefit as his.

"Hello, Aunt Miriam."

Little Stevie waved.

Miriam walked over with the puppy and placed him before the kids. "Where's your sister?"

Little Stevie rolled his eyes. "Where else?"

"With her boyfriend." Connie spoke the last word with a grimace.

Miriam shook her head. Little Stevie could be such a bad influence.

She glanced around. "Where's Cheri?"

"Uncle Nathan asked for her help. Sergeant Rizzo came for her a few hours ago."

"What does he want her for?"

Little Stevie shrugged.

"Sergeant Rizzo mentioned something about her helping to irrigate a prisoner."

Miriam forced down a laugh. "Do you mean interrogate?"

"Maybe that's it."

Miriam still harbored ill feelings toward Cheri. She and Badger had been captured by White Sands security when a Scavenger party attempted to retrieve the vehicles left behind during the ambush that had killed Steve. Cheri had soon come around to their way of thinking after realizing the propaganda Slade had told his people about White Sands had been lies. She had played a vital role in informing President Martinetti that the attack on Alamogordo was a diversion for the attempt to obtain a nuclear warhead at Kirtland, the operation that got Alissa and Chris killed and nearly did the same to Kiera. None of that was Cheri's fault. Ever since Nathan had assigned Cheri to this room so Miriam could keep an eye on her, the woman had watched Little Stevie and Connie when Miriam was at work and caused no problems. Cheri was just one of thousands of ordinary people whose lives had been irreversibly changed by the deader outbreak. Still, Miriam found it difficult to get over the fact that Cheri once belonged to the same group that had killed her husband.

She laid down and took a nap when the door opened. Cheri entered, accompanied by a young Japanese woman. Miriam went over to greet the newcomer.

"Who's the new person?"

Before Cheri could speak, Izumi smiled and offered her hand. "I'm Izumi."

Miriam refused to shake it. "Are you the Scavenger Abney and Lindsey brought back from Kirtland?"

"Yes." Izumi's smile faded.

"You're one of the people who almost killed my daughter."

Cheri attempted to intervene, but Izumi stood her ground. "Who was your daughter?"

"She was in the ambulance that you sideswiped with a dump truck. You broke her boyfriend's left arm and leg. She's lucky to be alive."

"Miriam," said Cheri. "Now's not the time or—"

"Yes, it is," interrupted Izumi. "A guy named Simpson drove the dump truck into the ambulance and caused those injuries. My friend So-young and I were guarding the entrance to the bunker from deaders when the firefight broke out. We went to investigate when your people fired on us, killing So-young. I'm sorry your daughter got caught up in this and was nearly killed. I really am. But I don't see anything sympathy from you about my friend. Nathan and Cheri have been trying to convince me that the people here at White Sands are better off than those at Vesta. Now I'm not so sure."

Thor ran over, glanced up at Miriam, thane rushed over to Izumi. He jumped up, placing his front paws on her knees, and barked.

"Hey there, little guy."

Thor's tail wagged and he barked again. Izumi picked up the dog and cuddled him, getting licked on the nose in return.

Cheri glared at Miriam, anger and confusion in her eyes.

Miriam could not blame her. Yes, she had a right to be furious that this conflict had killed Steve and almost did the same to Kiera. Slade waged this war. Everyone else merely fought the battles. Everyone in this room... everyone in both compounds... were ordinary people whose lives fell apart in a few days and who now did whatever was necessary to survive. Sure, Kiera could have been wounded at Kirtland. On the other hand, she could have been the one to shoot Izumi's friend.

Fuck this brave new world.

Izumi placed Thor on the floor and gave his butt a gentle pat, sending him scurrying back to Little Stevie and Connie.

"Take me back to my cell. I'm not welcome here."

"Yes, you are," said Miriam. "We've all lost friends and

loved ones since this began. We have to accept it and move on, otherwise we'll be fighting each other once the deaders are gone. I promise I won't give you any more trouble."

"Are you sure?" Cheri asked.

Miriam nodded.

Cheri ushered Izumi toward the back of the room. "My bunk is in back. You can take the top one."

Izumi paused by Miriam. "For what it's worth, I lost my husband and infant son on day three. He tried to get our baby out of the car seat when a pack of deaders ripped them to pieces. Every day since, I've had to live with the fact that I panicked and ran, saving my own life rather than dying trying to help them."

The two women headed for their bunk.

Realizing what was going on, Little Stevie picked up Thor. "Come on, Connie. Let's play outside for a while."

Miriam lay on her cot, pulled the blankets around her, and faced the wall to cry without being noticed. She silently sobbed for a few minutes when something jumped onto the mattress. Archer circled around her and rubbed his forehead against hers. The cat then curled about in a ball against her chest. Miriam dozed off to Archer's soothing purr.

Chapter Eleven

ALISSA AND O'BRIEN parked a mile away from the veterinary medical supply company. They stood by the front fender of the Sierra and studied the building through binoculars, occasionally checking the area around them to make sure no deaders snuck up on them. Shithead sat by Alissa's feet.

O'Brien lowered his binoculars. "This is turning out better than I thought."

Alissa agreed. Only one deader remained in the parking lot in front of the warehouse, stretched out on the asphalt with two broken legs. A sun-dried streak of congealed blood and bits of flesh ran for a hundred yards behind the thing from where it had dragged itself before finally giving up. The desert sun had desiccated the body. From this distance, it was impossible to tell whether it had any life left in it. Not that it mattered. It posed no threat.

The medical supply store sat in the center of the parking lot. No vehicles had been abandoned. No deaders roamed the area. The glass door and full-length windows leading into the store remained intact, a good sign that no one had ransacked the place.

"I can't believe our luck," said Alissa.

"I knew the owner. We used to get together for drinks on Friday nights. He put it out here in the middle of nowhere so junkies wouldn't break in and rob the place."

Alissa chuckled. "Of what? Flea and tick meds?"

"He kept a good supply of morphine and painkillers. It takes a lot of that stuff to make cattle feel better."

"I hate to break the glass to get inside."

"We don't have to. There are bay doors in the back. We'll sneak in that way. Let's go."

They climbed back into the Sierra and drove around back. The broken-legged deader raised its head as they passed and opened its mouth, its vocal cords too withered to snarl.

No deaders wandered around out back. The bay door remained closed, with the padlock securing it still in place.

"Looks quiet," said O'Brien.

The nurse in Alissa kicked in. "Don't say that."

"Why?"

"It's an old wives' tale among nurses. If you say it's quiet, then things are bound to go to shit."

"Sorry."

O'Brien backed the pickup to the bay door on the right, the one with the ramp. He left the engine running, got out, and removed a crowbar from the bed. Alissa followed as Shithead remained in the cab. O'Brien used the crowbar to snap off the padlock, then grabbed the handle. Alissa aimed her Mossberg 12-gauge shotgun in case any deaders were inside. O'Brien lifted the bay door.

The building was quiet.

"Anyone there?" called out O'Brien.

No response.

Alissa entered and checked the cargo bay for deaders while O'Brien backed the Sierra up the ramp. Once inside, he shut off the engine, closed the bay door, grabbed his .308 Winchester bolt-action hunting rifle and two high-powered flashlights from the front seat, and joined Alissa. He handed one of the flashlights to Alissa. Shithead jumped out of the cab and moved beside her.

"Ready?"

Alissa switched on her flashlight. "Let's do this."

NURSE ALISSA VS. THE ZOMBIES IX: CALM BEFORE THE STORM

They pushed open the swinging doors and entered the warehouse.

The putrid stench of decayed flesh wafted over them.

Alissa reached out and grabbed O'Brien by the forearm. "Do you smell that?"

"Deaders?"

She shrugged, then yelled, "Hello."

No response.

Alissa banged the stock of the shotgun against the metal door several times.

Still no response.

"Be careful and stay together just in case."

O'Brien nodded. "You don't have to tell me twice."

They made their way to the front of the store where the flatbed carts were kept. The closer they got, the more intense the stench became. By the time they reached the counter, the smell was overpowering. O'Brien leaned over the counter and checked the customer area but found nothing.

Shithead approached the manager's office on the left and whimpered. Alissa tapped O'Brien on the shoulder, placed a finger over her lips, then pointed to the office. The door sat ajar. The buzzing of insects came from inside. They raised their weapons into the high-ready position. Alissa stepped forward and pushed open the door. Disturbed by the movement, a swarm of flies flew around the room.

"Dear God," muttered O'Brien.

A body sat on a sleeping bag in one corner and propped up against the wall. It had long since decayed, leaving behind a puddle of putrefied flesh, tissues, and organs. A pile of empty food containers and bottled water stood in the opposite corner. A transistor radio rested on top of the desk and, beside it, a blue vest bearing the company's name and logo with a nametag attached that read FELICIA.

"What happened?" asked O'Brien. "Did she reanimate?"

Alissa shook her head. "She'd still be moving. It looks like she held up here with supplies hoping to ride out the apocalypse and died of starvation."

"Poor thing." O'Brien closed his eyes and said a silent prayer.

They left the office, Alissa closing the door behind her. O'Brien grabbed a flatbed cart and made his way through the store, stocking up on IV supplies, antibiotics, diabetes meds, and any other medical goods that might come in handy. It took less than fifteen minutes to gather what they needed.

O'Brien stretched. "There's a refrigerator unit at the back of the store. Let's check it out before we leave."

"Lead the way."

Unfortunately, the temperature gauge on the unit read seventy-one degrees.

"Damn it," O'Brien muttered.

"We tried. And we have what we came for, so let's not push our luck."

Once in the bay, they loaded their supplies into the back of the pickup. O'Brien pulled a tarpaulin over the bed and secured it in place.

"I'll start it. Can you get the door?"

"Sure."

Alissa went around to the front of the vehicle, grabbed the handle, and lifted the door.

Five coyotes waited for them on the ramp. Startled, four of them jumped back a few feet. The closest lunged, slamming into Alissa's chest and knocking her over. It went for her throat. She raised her left arm to block it, the animal sinking its teeth into her forearm. The coyote tugged on Alissa's arm, tearing at flesh and muscle. She cried out in pain.

Shithead dived out of the cab and went to help his mistress. He tackled the coyote, knocking it off Alissa and pinning it to the floor. The coyote tried to bite him, but Shithead dug his fangs into its neck and bit down, preventing the animal from getting to him.

O'Brien jumped out of the cab and used his rifle to take down the other four coyotes before they could regroup. Two died on the ramp. A third was wounded in its hindquarters and ran away, leaving a trail of blood. The fourth abandoned the pack and took off in another direction.

Alissa had gone through enough in the past several months to be ready for anything. She removed the revolver from its holster, placed the barrel against the coyote's temple, and pulled the trigger. Blood and brain matter splattered against the side of the pickup.

Alissa crawled over and hugged Shithead, who returned the gesture by giving her a face bath. She felt the dog for wounds. Thankfully, there were none. Alissa hugged him a second time.

"Good boy."

The dog smiled and barked.

O'Brien rushed over, took Alissa's good hand, and helped her up.

"Were they deaders?" he asked.

"I don't think so." Alissa glanced at the bodies on the ramp. "None of them looked as if they were reanimated. I think they were merely hungry and searching for food."

O'Brien led Alissa to the pickup and helped her into the passenger seat. Shithead climbed in over her and sat on the center seat. O'Brien opened the glove compartment, removed a roll of gauze and a tourniquet, and handed them to Alissa. As she tended to the wound, O'Brien picked up the body of the coyote that had attacked her and loaded it into the bed.

"What are you doing?"

"Bringing it back so Roni can check it for rabies."

Shit, thought Alissa. *Wouldn't that figure? I survived the deader apocalypse only to be taken out by a rabid animal. Fuck my luck.*

With the carcass loaded, O'Brien climbed into the driver's seat and shifted into drive. He drove down the ramp, crushing the bodies of the two dead coyotes, then went back to close the bay door and secure it with his own padlock. When finished, he jumped back behind the driver's seat.

"Do you need help?"

"I got this," Alissa replied as she finished wrapping the gauze around the wound. "I didn't hit an artery, or I'd be dead by now."

"Let's get you back and have Roni look at it."

Chapter Twelve

THE FIRST THING Roni did when Alissa and O'Brien returned to camp was to clean and dress her wound. It required twenty-three stitches. The bite was deep but had caused no permanent damage to the muscles. It would hurt for a few weeks, and Alissa would have an impressive scar on her arm but, other than that, she would be all right. Roni injected the area around the wound with Lidocaine and gave her a shot of Morphine to get through the initial bout of pain.

Next, she had O'Brien bring the coyote in from the truck and removed a piece of the animal's brain tissue to run a direct fluorescent antibody test to see if the animal had rabies. The results would not be ready for two hours. Roni assured Alissa she had nothing to worry about. Even if the coyote tested positive, she was well-equipped to handle it. All that would be required was four vaccine injections over the next two weeks.

Roni had taken Chris off the sedatives while Alissa and O'Brien were away. Since Alissa had been ordered to relax and favor the arm for the next twelve hours, she decided to sit with Chris in case he woke up.

Pulling a chair in from the corridor, Alissa placed it beside the bed and then sat down to rest, her feet propped on the mattress and her head resting against the wall. Shithead placed his front paws on the mattress, licked his master's face, then curled up beside the bed and napped.

Alissa reached out and squeezed Chris' hand. "Hang in there, love. We'll be back at White Sands soon."

Alissa dozed off within a few minutes.

She had no idea how long she had been asleep when a hand gently clasped hers. She opened her eyes. Chris stared at her and smiled.

"Hey, beautiful."

Alissa jumped out of the chair and embraced him. "I'm so glad you're okay."

"Who said I'm okay?" Chris rubbed her back. "My head feels like someone is tap dancing on it."

"That's because you have a mild concussion." Alissa broke the hug and stood, taking Chris' hands. "Roni says you'll be fine after a few days of bed rest."

"Who's Roni?"

"I'll explain later." She raised his hands to her lips and kissed the knuckles.

Chris' eyes widened in fear when he saw the blood-stained bandage wrapped around her left arm.

"Did one of those deaders in the bunker bite you?"

"No. A coyote did."

"I don't remember running into a coyote."

"Five of them. And you don't remember it because O'Brien and I dealt with them when we visited the veterinary supply store."

Chris stared at her, incredulous. "How long have I been out, and what did I miss? And while we're at it, where are we?"

Alissa laughed and held his hand. "You missed a lot."

She spent the next thirty minutes updating Chris on everything that had happened over the past few days, from the accident outside Kirtland until yesterday's raid for medical supplies. She finished describing the coyote attack as Roni entered.

"I'm glad to see you're awake. How do you feel?"

"Miserable, but at least I'll live."

"You can head back to White Sands in a few days." Roni turned her attention to Alissa. "And good news for you. The rabies test came back negative."

"Yes!" Alissa raised her fists in victory.

"I was concerned how the treatment might affect your baby."

Chris' eyes widened. "Baby?"

Alissa smiled awkwardly. "Yes."

"From what we did at Mass General?"

She nodded.

Roni became embarrassed. "I'll leave you alone."

Chris waited until they were alone. "Are you sure?"

"According to Roni, yes. It explains my throwing up so much. It's morning sickness."

Chris said nothing, an expression of shock on his face.

Alissa grew concerned. "You don't seem happy about this."

"I am." He smiled and took her hand. "I can't believe I'm going to be a father."

"You are."

Chris reached down and petted Shithead. "Here that, boy? You're going to have a brother."

Shithead's tail wagged. He turned to Alissa and barked.

"Why a brother?" asked Alissa. "It could be a girl."

"True. And if she's half the woman you are, she'll kick ass."

Alissa blushed.

O'Brien entered. "Sorry to disturb you, but I want to check on Chris. If everything is good, Roni wants to move him to the house tonight."

"House?" Chris glanced over at Alissa.

She stood and kissed him. "We'll talk more later. Now be a good boy and do as O'Brien tells you, otherwise I'll have to go into nurse mode on you."

Chris smiled and saluted. "Yes, ma'am."

Alissa left and returned to the house, feeling truly confident about the future for the first time in months.

Chapter Thirteen

"EXPLAIN TO ME again what we're doing?" Monica looked at the others, hoping for an answer.

"We have sixty-three people in the truck out there." Vince pointed to the smaller arrival pen where ten shamblers pressed against the sides, fingers stretched through the openings and decayed teeth chewing at the chain links. "The Boss wants us to use them to turn our prisoners into runners."

"Why don't we force them into the cage and let the deaders do what they do best?" asked Devon.

"Hey, asshole, I'm doing you a favor. If we let the prisoners get infected first, we have to transfer them from one cage to the other and arm them with the neck bombs. That poses a threat. If we arm them with the devices, let them get bit, then transfer them to the holding pen, they'll reanimate in there and lessen our chances of becoming infected."

"Makes sense," said Paul. "But how do we do that?"

Vince sighed in frustration, as if his team should be able to read minds. "We're going to bring them in three at a time, drug them, then prep them. If we work quickly enough, we'll have them collared up and loaded into the holding pen before any of them turn."

"We?" Terry asked snidely.

"Fuck you," Vince snapped. He spun around and headed for his office, pausing long enough to tell Carter, the head of the security team, "Get this shit underway."

Monica hoped she would be around when that fat son of a

bitch got what was coming to him.

Carter stepped forward, followed by his men. "Come on, people. The sooner we get this done, the sooner we can all get over to Big Jake's."

Everyone took their positions. Devon and the rest of his team stood by the bench a few yards from the entrance leading into the warehouse, the explosive collars waiting to be attached. Carter's men stood by the door, three holding a rag in one hand and a bottle of chloroform in the other, the fourth standing by as backup. Carter stepped outside.

A dozen of Mauler's team formed a semi-circle around the rear end of the tractor-trailer, their guns pointing to the ground but ready to be used at a moment's notice. Carter unlocked and lifted the sliding door to the trailer. Some of those inside screamed. Others moved closer to the front to avoid danger.

"What the fuck is going on here?" yelled a bearded man at the head of the crowd.

Carter raised his hands. "Calm down. Calm down."

The guards cocked their weapons. The gesture ended any further dissent.

"Listen," said Carter. "I know you're all scared. I promise nothing bad is going to happen to you."

"Why did you bring us here?" demanded an elderly man from the back.

"There was a swarm of deaders heading your way. I'm sorry our team was such assholes, but we're only trying to save you from being overrun."

"Did you have to shoot Reverend Moon?" asked a middle-aged woman in the back.

"That was unfortunate. The soldier who did that will be disciplined." More shouts were hurled at Carter. He ignored them and raised his hands again, waiting for the crowd to quiet down. "We'll answer all your questions later. Right now, I need to register you so we can assign you quarters. Okay?"

The crowd settled down.

"Thank you. We'll bring you in three at a time." Carter pointed to a young man, a young woman, and an older gentleman at the front of the group. "Follow me."

They hesitated, staring at each other with uncertainty.

"Please," Carter said in a friendly manner. "The quicker we get you registered, the quicker we can get you settled in."

The mock sincerity worked. The three walked down the ramp and followed Carter inside. The rest of the team stayed outside to guard the prisoners, trying not to look threatening.

"This will only take a few minutes. I'll get you some coffee while you wait."

"That would be awesome," replied the older gentleman.

Carter opened the door and ushered them inside.

Carter's team stepped up behind the prisoners and placed chloroform-laced rags over their faces. The young woman screamed, her cry muffled by the cloth. They struggled for a few seconds before going limp.

Devon's team ran up and took control. Monica, Renee, and Terry held up the prisoners while Devon, Eddie, and Paul attached the explosive collars around their necks. Throwing the prisoners' arms over their shoulders, two team members per prisoner, they dragged the limp bodies over to the cage with the shamblers inside. The living dead grew increasingly agitated as they approached. Devon's people stopped two feet from the cage. Monica, Renee, and Terry held out the right arms of the perspective prisoners and pushed the fingers between the chain links. The shamblers lunged, snapping at the extended digits, in most cases biting off the fingers. Once the prisoners had been infected, they were dragged across the warehouse into the holding pen and laid down at the far end. On the way out, Devon secured the inner gate.

Renee studied the three prisoners. "Won't they turn and attack us while we try to load in the others?"

"No," answered Monica. "The chloroform will keep them unconscious for a while."

"She's right," agreed Devon. "Let's hurry."

Renee joined the others back at the workbench. Devon turned to Carter and nodded. Carter left to get three more prisoners.

The process continued for close to an hour and, for the most part, proceeded smoothly. Most prisoners succumbed easily. A few struggled but only for a few seconds. One burly guy with a beard fought back. The fourth guard placed a stun gun against the back of the burly guy's neck and pulled the trigger, ending it quickly. They had processed forty-two prisoners and were working on the next three when Murphy's Law came into effect.

Paul and Renee dragged a young, muscled man with a crew cut to the arrival pen and stuck his fingers through the links. When one of the shamblers bit into his forefinger, the man woke up and jerked his arm back. The finger tore off in the deader's mouth. His elbow slammed into Renee's face, shattering her nose. She cried out and released her grip. With his right hand free, the young man grabbed Renee by the back of the hair and shoved her face against the chain links. The shamblers broke into a feeding frenzy and attacked. The fourth guard raced over, shoved the stun gun against the prisoner's head, and pulled the trigger, the electric bolt dropping the man instantly. He released his grip on Renee, who jumped away from the cage.

"Shit," mumbled Monica.

Renee's nose had been chewed off, and she had teeth marks on her right cheek. Blood flowed down her face. She wiped her hand across the skin and stared at it, her eyes widening in terror.

"Th-they're minor wounds," she pleaded. "I'll be okay, right?"

None of the team responded.

"Right?"

Paul shook his head. "You're infected."

"No!" Renee screamed the word. "Please, you can't let me become one of those things. Kill me."

The team was still too much in shock to reply.

Renee turned to the guards. "Shoot me!"

Carter took the stun guard from the fourth guard and stepped forward. Renee dropped to her knees and closed her eyes, whispering to him, "Thank you."

Instead of removing his revolver and placing a bullet through Renee's head, he used the stun gun against her chest. She cried out for a second and collapsed.

"That's not enough to kill her," advised Monica.

"I didn't intend to kill her. Put a collar on her and throw her in with the others."

"She's one of us," Devon protested.

"Not anymore." Carter stepped up to Devon and got in his face. "There's nothing we can do for her. She'll be a deader in a few hours. I know it sucks. Since we can't help her, at least we can use her as part of the bomb team."

Devon disagreed but refused to argue.

"Prepare her," Carter ordered. When no one responded, he yelled. "Do it now, or you'll all join her."

The other guards straightened up and glared at Devon's team, letting them know their boss was serious.

Finally, Devon caved in. "Monica, put a collar on Renee and help me move her to the cage."

"And hurry up," ordered Carter. "We still have twenty-one prisoners to process."

Six more sets of prisoners were brought in to be sedated, equipped with an explosive collar, bitten by deaders, and tossed into the holding pen. As the guards headed for the exit, Carter yelled to the others, "We're almost done. Only three left."

"Thank Christ," mumbled Paul. "This sucks."

"What do you mean?" asked Eddie. "We've done this dozens of times."

"On deaders. This time we're doing it to the living. It's

murder."

Devon looked at his friends. "What choice do we have?"

"We could refuse to do it," offered Monica.

Paul glared at her. "I don't see you standing up to them."

Monica lowered her gaze. For all her bluster, she was as terrified as the others over what would happen if she protested and—

Terry gasped. "Oh, fuck no."

Everyone glanced over at Terry, who had an expression of disgust on her face. They followed her eyes to the door leading outside. Monica wanted to vomit.

Carter had brought in the last three prisoners—a young girl approximately five years old, a boy not much older, and a Korean girl barely in her teens. Carter's three guards covered their mouths with rags, rendering the children unconscious. No one on Devon's team moved.

Carter stepped in front of the prisoners. "What the fuck are you waiting for?"

"We can't," said Monica. "They're children."

"You can and you will. If my men have to do it, we'll add you to the pen."

To emphasize his point, the fourth guard moved to one side of Carter, swung his weapon off his shoulder, and aimed it at Devon's team.

A tense few seconds elapsed before Paul sighed. "Let's get this over with."

Terry shook her head. "Damn it, Paul. They're kids."

"They're going to be turned anyways. I don't want to join them." The others felt the despair in Paul's eyes.

Carter sneered. "You better listen to him, bitch."

"I hate you all." Terry joined the others.

It took only a few minutes to attach the explosive collars, drag the children to the arrival pen to be bitten, and then place them in the holding pen. As Paul closed and secured the twin doors to the cage, the first of the infected prisoners rose to their feet as the living dead, snarling at those on the other side of the chain links.

As Paul's team was cleaning up, Carter joined them. "I know what you all did was rough. Believe me, it bothered us."

"You didn't show it," snapped Terry.

Carter ignored her. "Leave this shit for tomorrow and come over to Big Jake's. Drinks are on me. We all deserve to get hammered tonight."

"I'll take you up on that," said Paul, his tone lacking emotion.

The two teams exited the warehouse. Once in the office, Vince looked up from his desk where he was reading an old issue of *Hustler*.

"It took you long enough."

"Fuck off," said Carter as he and his team stored their weapons in the lockers. "You never help us out."

"Because I'm the boss, asshole. You guys do all the work."

Carter ignored him. "We'll be back tomorrow to clean the place up."

Vince started to argue but thought better of it.

Both teams left the warehouse and headed for Big Jake's. Terry walked slower than the others and quickly fell behind. Monica joined her.

"Are you okay?"

"Of course, I'm not fucking okay! I just helped murder sixty-three people, including three kids. You shouldn't be either."

"Sorry."

"No, you're not." Terry broke away and walked in another direction.

"Where are you going?"

"I need to be alone for a while."

Monica did not blame her. She hated herself. To survive, she had become as cruel and heartless as the rest of the teams. She planned on drinking tonight until she passed out, hoping to sleep without having nightmares over what she had done. It would only be a temporary solution. Today would haunt her for the rest of her life.

At that moment, Monica decided to escape at the first opportunity, even if the attempt killed her.

Chapter Fourteen

N ATHAN ENTERED THE infirmary to provide another round of blood samples for Carrington to create the vaccine. He did not mind giving blood for the cause. It was the process that proved aggravating. So many needles had been jabbed into his left elbow, and so many vials of blood removed that he had developed a bruise the size of an egg on his left antecubital. The damn thing hurt every time he flexed his lower arm. During the last visit, Carrington had switched over and began using the veins in his right elbow. Soon, his right arm would be hurting whenever he moved it. On the plus side, per the doctor's orders, he received a lot of red meat whenever he went to the mess hall to help replenish his blood supply.

A small price to pay for providing the military with the means to fight deaders and take back the planet.

Nathan made his way to the lab where Emily, one of the nurse practitioners, greeted him with a smile.

"That time again?"

"Sadly, yes."

"Have a seat. I'll be with you in a minute."

Nathan slid into the phlebotomy chair, swung out the extending arm, rolled up his right sleeve, and rested his arm on it.

Emily came over a few seconds later with a needle and five empty vials. "You're getting good at this."

"I've done this so many times that I'm probably qualified to take my own blood samples."

"Trust me, I've tried. It's not as easy as you think." She

studied his arm. "Still bruised on the left side?"

"It looks like a rotting avocado."

Emily wrapped a tourniquet around his upper arm, pulled it tight, then wiped down his antecubital with an alcohol pad and inserted the needle. Nathan winced, more from the bruise than the injection. Emily inserted the first vial.

"How much longer will I have to do this?"

"Until Dr. Acula says he has enough samples."

It took Nathan a few seconds to get the joke. He watched Emily switch out the vials one by one. When finished, she withdrew the needle, placed a piece of gauze over it, and had Nathan hold it. Emily attached a bandage over the gauze.

"Thanks." Nathan started to stand. "I'll see you tomorrow."

"Dr. Carrington asked me to keep you here. He wants to talk with you."

That cannot be good, thought Nathan. "What about?"

Emily shrugged. "He doesn't tell us anything. He'll be here in a minute to talk with you. See you tomorrow."

When she left, Nathan leaned back, rested his head against the wall, and closed his eyes. Less than a minute later, Carrington entered.

"Sorry, did I wake you?"

"Nope." Nathan sat up in the chair. "What did you want to see me about?"

"We've taken a lot of blood out of you. I wanted to make sure you're feeling okay."

"I feel fine. Just a little tired."

"That's normal." Carrington removed a blood pressure monitor from his pocket and slid it over Nathan's right arm. "Any dizziness?"

"No."

"Shortness of breath?"

"No."

"That's good." Carrington inflated the blood pressure cuff

until it tightened around Nathan's upper arm, then slowly released the pressure. After a few seconds, the doctor deflated the cuff and removed it from Nathan's arm. "It's 118/76. Pretty good."

"That means I'm in for more bloodletting."

"Not as much as you think. I've tested Badger's blood, and it'll work as a base for a vaccine, so we've started drawing samples from him. That will take some of the pressure off you."

"He must be thrilled."

"Screw him. At least he's now of some use to the compound." Carrington motioned for Nathan to roll down his sleeve. "We won't be taking blood from you for a few days. Give you a chance to rest up."

"Thanks." Nathan rolled down his shirt sleeve and stood. "Does this mean Badger gets my steaks for the next few days?"

"No way. The steaks are still reserved for you." Carrington chuckled, which was uncharacteristic. "He's getting nothing but MREs until his attitude improves."

"Don't hold your breath." Nathan left the lab, pausing long enough to add, "See you in a few days."

MALCOLM SLAMMED SHUT the cover of his laptop, rested his elbow on the counter, and massaged his forehead. By now, he should have figured out how the signal to detonate the neck bombs worked but still drew a blank. It had to be the concussion and the pain meds he was taking. They dulled his mind. At this rate, he would never figure out how to counter Slade's suicide deaders. The worst part, he was letting down the others.

He kicked the counter's front panel. The shock sent a wave of pain through his healing arm and leg.

"That's not like you," came a soothing voice behind him.

Malcolm shifted on his stool. Kiera crossed the lab, wrapped her arms around Malcolm's good one, and kissed him.

"What's wrong, hon?"

"I'm what's wrong." He leaned his head against her shoulder. "I can't figure out the code to the triggering device."

"You've been through a lot the past few days."

"My body is banged up, not my mind."

Kiera raised an eyebrow. "You have a concussion, remember?"

"That doesn't matter. I need to figure this out and can't. I'm useless."

"You're far from useless. But I'm not going to argue with you." Kiera brought over his wheelchair, helped him into it, and led him across the lab.

"What are you doing? I'm in no shape for that."

"That's not what I'm after, dork. I need to show you something."

"What?"

"Follow me."

Kiera led Malcolm outside. A golf cart waited by the entrance. She helped transferred him in and slid into the driver's seat.

"Moving is a pain in the ass," Malcolm complained. "This better be good."

"Oh, it is."

They drove to the motor pool. Malcolm's eyes widened when Kiera circled around to the back of the garage.

"That's friggin' awesome."

"I knew you'd want to see it."

The carpool staff had removed one of the gatling guns from an A-10. More accurately, they had taken the aircraft off the weapon, discarding the fuselage and engines. They then mounted it on the rear of the Tatra AD 20 truck the desert runners had discovered earlier at the junkyard, the gatling gun being substituted for the crane.

The weapon was massive. The magazines were larger than

a Volkswagen Beetle. Each of the seven barrels measured seven feet long. Malcolm once read that the A-10 served as a platform to move the cannon around. He now realized the accuracy of that statement.

Several people stood in a small group by the Tatra. Malcolm noticed President Martinetti and her chief of staff; Colonel Roberts; Nathan; Abney and Lindsey; and Izumi and Cheri, who served as the president's advisor on the Scavengers. Kiera parked the golf cart beside them.

Martinetti stepped over and offered her hand. "I assume you're Malcolm?"

"I am."

"This was a brilliant idea on your part."

"Thank you, Madam President." Malcolm beamed with pride. "I figured these guns would stop anything Slade uses against us."

"Gun," corrected the colonel. "The barrels of the second one were damaged and couldn't be fixed, though we were able to salvage the ammo."

"One should be enough to stop him."

"Maybe," said Jill. "Can they stop an armored car?"

"That's why you're here," countered Roberts with a smug grin. "For a demonstration."

The weapon was aimed at an M1 Abrams parked in the desert.

"Is it worth destroying one of our tanks to make a point?" asked Martinetti.

"That one has a bad transmission. We stripped everything of value out of it to use on the other Abrams."

Roberts turned to the lieutenant standing by the gatling gun and signaled for him to proceed. The officer fired a rapid burst lasting five seconds, releasing three hundred and fifty 30mm rounds. The staccato buzz of the spinning barrels drowned out the sound of each round tearing into the tank. Jill grimaced and covered her ears. A cloud of smoke formed around the M1 and hung there for several seconds after the gatling gun ceased. When it finally cleared, the Abrams had scores of holes punched through its armor. The tread along the left side had been torn to pieces, and the road wheels shattered as if they were China plates. The gun barrel had dislodged from its mounting and hung limply across the glacis plate, the front three feet of the barrel having been blasted off and tossed several yards away. Only a smoldering wreck remained.

Roberts turned to Jill. "Satisfied?"

The chief of staff nodded, embarrassed at having been shown up.

Nathan turned to Izumi. "Does Slade have any tanks or armored vehicles at his disposal?"

She shook her head. "The two biggest vehicles he had were the truck that carries the suicide deaders and the fire engine, and you destroyed that at Kirtland. Other than that, he has an old-style military transport, a few Hummers, and some civilian vehicles."

Roberts nodded. "We're ready for anything Slade throws against us."

"I'd love to use one of those on a horde of deaders," joked Abney.

"It would be fun to watch," agreed the colonel. "But it would be a terrible waste of resources."

"What if Slade tries to swarm White Sands and overrun our defenses?" asked Martinetti. "Could we use it then?"

The colonel thought about it. "I guess as a last resort."

"Jesus," Lindsey said, despair in her voice. "That would be a slaughter."

"It's us or them," responded Martinetti, stating the obvious.

"There may be another way to stop that," said Malcolm.

Martinetti glanced over at him. "Go on."

"The problem is if Slade decides to use a horde of deaders or his own people to launch a swarm attack on the compound, right?"

"Yes."

"And given how long the perimeter stretches around White Sands, there's no way we can be everywhere at once."

Martinetti nodded.

"What if we try this?"

Malcolm spent the next six minutes explaining his idea to the president. When finished, he noticed everyone staring at him. Did he overextend his hand?

"That's ridiculous," blurted Jill.

"It is," replied Martinetti. "But it might work. Colonel, can we implement it within a week?"

Roberts thought for a moment. "Not for all of White Sands, but we could easily arrange it to protect the main compound. I'll have my men start on it later tonight."

"Where will we get so many deaders?" asked Jill.

Martinetti stared at her chief of staff, incredulous.

"In Alamogordo," Lindsey replied. "They're already stirred up by the Scavengers' raid the other day. Drawing them out will be easy."

Martinetti focused on the colonel. "How do you propose to round them up?"

"Slade used a tractor-trailer," offered Izumi.

"How did he do that?" asked Abney.

"Someone would lure the deaders into the trailer, climb a ladder to the roof, then close the sliding door behind them."

Nathan laughed.

"What's so funny?" asked the president.

"I have just the person for that job."

"Then do it. I want a daily briefing on our progress."

Roberts nodded. "Yes, Madam President."

Martinetti walked over to the golf cart. "Once this whole nightmare with Slade is over, I want you to join my staff as my scientific advisor."

"Are you serious?"

"Have you ever known me not to be serious?"

"It'd be an honor."

"Good." Martinetti leaned to the side and locked eyes with Kiera. "Take good care of Malcolm. I need him."

"We all do." Kiera smiled and patted Malcolm's good leg.

Martinetti turned to Nathan. "I want you to work with the colonel to implement Malcolm's plan."

"Yes, ma'am."

The president and Jill entered their Jeep and returned to the Oval Office.

Roberts walked up to the cart and nodded at Malcolm. "I'll send over some of my people in an hour so you can figure out the best places to lay these traps."

"Not a problem." Malcolm tapped his casts. "I'm not going anywhere."

Roberts smiled and patted Malcolm on his shoulder. "Good job, kid."

When the colonel had departed, Abney and Lindsey joined them.

"Well," said Lindsey, "it looks like we're losing our whiz kid."

"I knew one day we'd be proud of him," joked Abney.

"One day?" Malcolm chuckled.

"I'm always proud of you." Kiera leaned over and kissed Malcolm on his cheek.

"Be proud all you want. I still have to crack the code for the neck bombs."

"Excuse me, guys." Kiera grinned. "I have to get our little genius back to the lab."

Chapter Fifteen

A LISSA AND RONI scrubbed up for the operation on Mr. Spritzer. Earlier that morning, the two of them helped O'Brien bleach the operating room in the vet clinic and set up everything for this morning's procedure. O'Brien scrubbed up earlier and brought Mr. Spritzer over, staying with him until the two women showed up.

"It's been a while since I've done surgery," Alissa said in passing.

"It's one of those things you never forget, like riding a bike. Only a little more complicated." Roni paused. "Are you up to doing this?"

"If you're asking if I'm nervous, no. I'm anxious to get back in the operating room. I miss it."

"What about your arm?"

Alissa flexed her fingers. "It hurts like hell, but I can still use it. I'll be fine."

"I'll give you some painkillers afterward."

"Thanks."

When finished, they entered the operating room. O'Brien waited near the entrance and helped them slip on their surgical gloves. They approached the table where Mr. Spritzer lay. His face lit up on seeing them.

"I must have died and gone to Heaven because I see angels."

Roni tapped his hand. "You're not going to heaven today. This is a simple procedure. When you wake up, you'll feel much better."

"But I'll only have one leg."

"It's better than dying," Alissa tried to comfort him.

"I'm not complaining. I only wish I was a girl."

Both women stared at him. "Why?"

"Then you could call me Eileen."

Alissa chuckled. At first, Roni did not get it. When she did, she sighed and rolled her eyes.

As Alissa chatted amiably with Mr. Spritzer to distract him, Roni inserted an IV needle connected to a saline bag, then attached the leads and sensors to the intraoperative monitor for his vital signs. When finished, she nodded to Alissa that they were ready.

"Let me give you a hug for good luck." Alissa leaned over the bed.

"I'll always take a hug from a pretty lady."

Mr. Spritzer wrapped his left arm around and embraced her. When Alissa stood up, he was sound asleep.

"How are his vitals?" Roni asked.

"All good."

"Let's begin."

Moving to either side of the operating table, the two women began the procedure. O'Brien tightly wrapped a tourniquet around the thigh to stop blood flow, sterilized the area to be operated on with an antibacterial solution, and moved down to end of the table.

Roni proceeded with a transtibial amputation seventeen centimeters below Mr. Spritzer's knee. Using a scalpel, she made anterior and posterior incisions around the leg, beginning with shallow cuts into the skin and then slowly going deeper. Alissa assisted by placing a pair of retractors on either side of the leg, hooking the ends around the tissue on the upper leg and keeping it elevated. Roni made the cut inches at a time until the fibula and tibia were exposed.

With both bones cleared of tissue, Roni began the osteotomy of the fibula. Using a bone saw, she cut the fibula two centimeters below the incision as O'Brien cooled the circular blade with saline. Once she detached the fibula, Roni used a curette to scrape the muscles and tissues off the tibia, then used the saw to cut through that bone.

"Thank God."

"What?" asked Alissa.

"None of the narcosis has moved this far up the leg. I was afraid muscular deterioration might have advanced farther than on the surface."

Roni placed the severed lower leg on a nearby table to be disposed of later as Alissa removed the retractors. Finding the critical neurovascular structures, Roni performed ligation of the arteries first, tying the ends closed with sutures. For the veins, she used rat-toothed forceps to pull the tissue aside and hemostatic forceps to pull out the ends of the veins a few millimeters, keeping the forceps' tips clamped around the veins. One by one, Alissa turned them over so Roni could tie a suture around the end of the vein and then, when Alissa removed the forceps, tied it a second time and cut off the extra length.

"Release the tourniquet."

O'Brien moved up alongside Alissa and removed it. Blood slowly dripped from the severed leg.

"Do you want me to reapply it?" O'Brien asked.

"No. That's normal."

Roni began the Targeted Muscle Reinnervation portion of the surgery, attaching the severed nerves to muscles so they would regenerate in an organized fashion.

"Will you be fitting him with a prosthetic?" asked Alissa.

"No. I'm doing this to prevent neuromas and phantom limb pain."

With the nerves reattached, Roni sliced away the skin around the wound and musculature, then removed any excess muscle. She tied the remaining muscles with purse-string style suturing, sealing off the amputated bones. The final portion of the operation involved cleaning excess fat and skin away from the flaps until she could close off the open area with no excess muscle or skin. She then administered a dose of prophylactic antibiotics.

"Now comes the easy part."

"What's that?" asked O'Brien.

"Wrapping it with gauze," Alissa replied.

The entire procedure lasted three hours. When finished, O'Brien wheeled Mr. Spritzer into one of the nearby rooms and would wait with him until the anesthesia wore off. Alissa and Roni exited the OR, stripping off their blood-covered clothes and tossing them into a waste basket to be washed later.

Alissa leaned against the counter and sighed, tired from the surgery. "You did well in there."

"For a vet?"

"No, I mean as a surgeon. I knew doctors at Mass General who didn't work as professionally as you did."

"Thanks." Roni smiled. "Time will tell how good I was. If I cleaned out the excess muscles properly, the tissue should grow back normally. If I screwed it up, an infection could set in. I doubt he'd survive that."

"Let's worry about that *if* it happens." Alissa stretched, twisting her upper body from side to side to work out the kinks. "What now?"

"O'Brien will stay with Mr. Spritzer until he wakes up and will get him settled. As for you and me, we're going back to the house for a drink. I think we earned it."

Chapter Sixteen

T HIS WAS MALCOLM'S most tedious task since attending Algebra 1 in high school. He mounted the detonation device for the neck bombs on a workbench on the opposite side of the room, the green light facing him. Seated at his station, he set the frequency on his transmitter and sent a signal, starting with the lowest frequencies and working his way up to the extremely high ones. If the green light on the detonator lit up, then he found the proper frequency. So far, after several hours of trying, it had not. The radio spectrum was huge, ranging from one Hertz to three thousand Gigahertz. And he had only worked his way through less than a quarter of the available frequencies. Malcolm felt like he was chasing a rabbit down a hole that wound its way across New Mexico and Arizona.

Making the monotony even worse was the incessant itching under the two casts. He remembered watching his friend in middle school unwinding a coat hanger and using the end to scratch beneath it, thinking the kid was insane and would tear up his skin. Now that he went through the same thing, Malcolm wanted to floss the area between his skin and the cast with barbed wire.

Shaking his head to shift his attention back onto the task at hand, Malcolm switched to the next frequency, pressed the button on the transmitter, and cursed under his breath when nothing happened.

"No wonder you can't get anything done," Kiera said from behind him. "You probably shook your brain loose."

"Being brain dead would help with the boredom."

"I can fix that."

Kiera wrapped her arms around his neck and kissed him deeply. The hug hurt his broken arm, but Malcolm would not complain. After a few seconds, Kiera broke the embrace, pulled a stool over to the workbench, and sat beside him.

"Can I help?"

"Thanks, but there's not much you can do." Malcolm used his right hand to move the frequency up one notch. "It's time-consuming going through every frequency available looking for the right one."

He pressed the button to send a signal. Nothing happened.

Malcolm huffed.

Kiera pulled the notebook to Malcolm's left over to her and read it. Close to a hundred frequencies were jotted down in bad penmanship.

"You haven't gone through that many."

Malcolm switched to the next frequency. "That's not all of them. Every fifteen minutes, I jot down the last one I used. That way, if something happens, I don't have to start over."

He pressed the transmit button. When nothing happened, he changed frequency again.

"Let's take a break." Kiera gently rubbed his back. "You need to get away from this and clear your head."

"I don't have time." Malcolm continued the process. Nothing. "For all we know, Slade will attack us tonight or tomorrow."

"You won't be any good if you're too tired to function. Come on. We'll grab lunch and take a nap."

"You mean breakfast."

"It's almost noon."

Malcolm checked his watch. Damn, he had been at this all morning and lost track of time. Kiera was right. He needed a break. He switched to the next frequency.

"Write this number down for me."

"Sure." Kiera grabbed a pen, recorded the frequency Malcolm read to her, and then placed the clipboard on the workbench. "Are you ready?"

"Yeah." Malcolm pressed the transmit button and gasped.

"What's wrong?"

He pointed to the detonator. The light shown bright green.

"Does that mean what I think it does?" asked Kiera.

"It does." Malcolm looked at her, his demeanor filled with excitement. "We can blow up Slade's suicide deaders whenever we want."

Chapter Seventeen

ZACH STARED AT the interior of the W88 warhead, completely at a loss as to what to do next. He had removed the nose cone shield earlier that morning to study the device. This warhead had been configured to detonate at a certain height above its designated target, generating an airburst that would create the maximum damage. Finding the barometric pressure sensor that triggered the warhead at its proper altitude was easy. Removing it had also been a simple procedure. However, Zach had no idea how to proceed.

"This is ridiculous," he mumbled to himself.

"What is?" Tara placed down the neck bomb she worked on.

"I'm stuck. I don't know where to go from here. If I don't figure it out, Slade is going to hand our asses to us."

"Maybe that's a good thing."

Zach's expression went from frustration to disbelief. "Are you serious?"

"If you figure out how to detonate that thing, Slade will use it on White Sands. Thousands will die. Those who survive will be brought back here and either used as suicide deaders or thrown into the back room of Big Jake's. Do you want to be responsible for that?"

Zach did not want to respond because he knew he would not like his answer, so he diverted the question. "If I don't do this, Slade will throw you back in the rape room., if he doesn't kill you first."

"I don't care. I'd rather either of those options than live with the fact that I'm responsible for murdering so many people and ruining the lives of those who survive." Tara slid off her work stool, crossed the lab, and moved beside Zach. Her eyes locked on his. "Are you willing to live with it?"

Rage flared inside Zach. Then he realized the anger was directed not at Tara but himself for not having the courage to stand up to Slade. He turned away and went back to studying the warhead.

Zach flinched when Tara gently placed her hand on his shoulder. Rather than continue the argument, she rubbed her palm down his back.

"What are you stuck on?"

Tara did not deserve him. She should be with someone with enough integrity to do the right thing.

"Come on, baby. Maybe I can help."

Zach tamped down his self-loathing. "This warhead had a sensor attached that would detonate it once it reached a set altitude. I removed the sensor but can't figure out how to set up the trigger for remote detonation."

"Can't they be set off with a timer? I saw Bruce Willis do it in that movie where they had to blow up the asteroid before it hit earth. We set it to go off in ten minutes, drop off the warhead at its target, and get out of the area before it goes off."

Zach smiled. At least Tara tried.

"What's so funny?"

"Nothing. You're adorable, that's all."

Tara rolled her eyes. "Thanks. But does my idea make sense?"

"It does, but I ruled it out already."

"Why?"

"Whoever places the device would need several minutes to get far enough away so he wouldn't be killed in the blast. In that time, anyone at White Sands could move it to a spot where the distance diminished its effects. This only works if I can figure out how to detonate the warhead remotely once it's in place. The problem is, I can't."

Tara considered the options. "What if you used a timer, set it for… I don't know… ten seconds. And then used a remote control to start the timer. That way, you would have more control over when it goes off."

"What type of timer?"

Tara shrugged. "I don't know. You're the tech genius."

"I'm far from a genius."

"I remember reading once that during the Iraq War, terrorists used cellphones to trigger their IEDs."

"You're the genius." Zach took Tara's cheeks in his hands and kissed her.

"You're going to use a cellphone to detonate the warhead?"

"No. The reception is too spotty out here. Besides, cellphones are unreliable." Zach went over to a shelf against the wall, pulled out a cardboard box with the word JUNK scrawled across the front in black magic marker, and rummaged through it. "I need a radio transmitter and receiver. I think I have some… Yes."

He removed a pair of two-way radios and showed them to Tara.

"I don't get it."

"I can use these to set up the long-distance remote by adapting them to transmit a signal on a frequency that can't be blocked." The more Zach talked, the more animated he became. He held up one radio and then the other. "Slade presses a button on one of these, and the other detonates the warhead. It's so simple I never even thought of it."

"I'm the one with the simple mind, so I thought of it." Tara meant it as a joke, but her tone had a tint of shame.

Zach focused on her. "You're not simple. You're special."

Tara rolled her eyes. "That makes me feel a lot better."

"That's not what I meant." Zach left the radios on the workbench and walked over to Tara, lovingly placing his hands on her upper arms. "I have so many ideas running through my head that I'm practically bouncing off the walls in the lab. You've done something no one has ever been able to do before. You keep me grounded. You make me remember what's important in life. I love you for that."

Zach took Tara in his arms and held her close for several seconds before breaking the embrace. He then checked his watch.

"It's almost dinner. Let's grab a bite to eat and come back here to spend some time alone. We can work on this later tonight."

Chapter Eighteen

"How's it going?" asked Roberts.

Nathan did not hear him because of the irritating blare of the backhoe's reverse signal.

"How's it going?" This time the colonel yelled the question.

Nathan turned and held up his hand until the backhoe stopped. "We're making progress. Let me show you."

The two men moved closer to the trenches currently being worked on by construction crews in the glare of a string of lumen work lights. Roberts had decided to establish the trench system two miles from the compound. That way, if Slade made it close enough to detonate the warhead, it would do minimal damage. It was a compromise. Setting up the perimeter any closer would give them a better ring of protection but would cause more destruction if the device went off. At this distance, damage from the blast would be minimal, but that meant leaving sections of the perimeter unprotected.

Nathan stood in the center of the road leading from the north gate along Route 380 to the compound. Two trenches one hundred feet long, ten feet wide, and ten feet deep extended on either side of the road. The excess sand was distributed behind the trenches, forming defensive positions, or formed into a semi-circular berm in the road blocking access and providing the M1s with a covered position from which to fire.

"So far, we've established one of these roadblocks on every road leading to the compound."

Roberts examined the berm and the trenches. "Impressive."

"Thanks. Now we're going to start connecting them."

"Will you have enough time to complete the project?"

"Doubtful, unless Slade doesn't launch his attack for a few weeks. We'll dig trenches three hundred feet long halfway between each roadblock and, when those are completed, a second set between them. We'll keep doing that until we've completed the perimeter. If not, then at least we'll have defensive positions evenly placed across the desert."

"It looks like you have everything under control."

"Thanks."

The colonel stopped at one of the trenches and examined it. "What about the deaders?"

"Abney and Lindsey have figured out a way to gather and safely transport them onto base. We're going to implement the plan later this morning."

"If anyone can do it, it'll be you three."

"Thanks. Do you want to see the other roadblocks?"

"I'm good." The two walked back to the colonel's Humvee. "Keep me informed of the progress. And let me know if you need anything."

"I will."

Nathan watched the colonel drive off and then checked his watch. He needed to get to the infirmary to arrange the critical part of the operation.

Chapter Nineteen

THE CORRIDOR LIGHTS in the infirmary were dimmed as Nathan entered. Not that it surprised him. It was only 0635, and the unit had yet to switch over to dayshift. He wanted to get to Alamogordo around sunrise and give his team the advantage.

As he neared the nurse's station, he spotted Jessica manning the desk. She looked up upon hearing him, broke into a huge smile, and pushed a lock of brunette hair behind her ear.

"Hello, Man Who Saved the World. My shift ends in twenty-five minutes. Did you come to take me to breakfast?"

"I can't today."

"You're trying to say no in a nice way. I get it."

"That's not it." Nathan knew how to handle any situation involving deaders. Dealing with Jessica made him nervous. "I have an operation this morning."

"Likely story."

"It's true. Please, believe me. I'd love nothing more than to take you to breakfast. But today, I can't."

"I know." Jessica chuckled and pulled the square-rimmed Versace glasses down her nose. "I'm teasing you. Sergeant Rizzo and Private Barnes showed up five minutes ago and are waiting at Badger's room for you."

Nathan stared at her, stunned.

"It worked. I got a commitment from you for another date." Jessica gave him a smile filled with sexual innuendoes. "And I'm holding you to that."

"I'm a man of my word."

Nathan made his way to Badger's room. Rizzo and Barnes had replaced the night shift guards and waited for him. Rizzo glanced over and nodded. "Morning, sir."

"I'm not military. Call me Nathan."

"Yes, sir."

He sighed. "Is our friend ready?"

"We haven't checked on him yet. But the previous shift said he's normal."

"You mean he's being a pain in the ass."

"You got it."

"Are we going to let deaders bite him again?" asked Barnes.

"Not intentionally. Let's do this."

Nathan opened the door to Badger's room and entered. The prisoner lay sound asleep. Nathan picked up the rolling stool, raised it in front of him, and dropped it on the floor. The loud clang jolted Badger awake. He sat up, grimacing as the handcuffs around his wrists pulled tight against the sidebars. A second later, he noticed Nathan and the guards standing there.

"What the fuck? Why'd you wake me?"

"It's time to get up."

"You could have done it nicer."

"You can give me a bad review on Yelp. We have somewhere to go."

Badger extended his middle finger.

"That's not nice," Nathan responded with a smirk.

"What are you going to do? Have another deader bite me?"

"That's not part of the plan."

Some of the defiance drained out of Badger. "What plan?"

"You'll find out." Nathan turned to Rizzo. "Uncuff him. If he gives you shit, tase him."

"Does it matter where?" asked Barnes.

"As long as you don't kill him."

Rizzo uncuffed Badger from the bed and then secured his

hands behind him as Barnes tapped the barrel of the taser against his hand. When finished, they led Badger out of the hospital, placed him in a golf cart, and headed for the motor pool. Badger blustered the entire time until they arrived at their destination. He suddenly became more docile.

"What the fuck is that?"

"That" referred to an old school bus decked out so it looked like something from a *Mad Max* movie. Two Bradley Fighting Vehicles sat near it with ten soldiers geared up for combat waiting around the lowered back doors. Abney, Lindsey, Izumi, and Cheri stood by the RAM.

"That's your ride."

"Ride where?"

"Into Alamogordo." Nathan stopped the golf cart, got out, and headed for the bus.

"Why the fuck are we going there? That place is infested with deaders. Hey! Answer me."

Badger's protesting ended when the two guards uncuffed him and led him to the bus. Abney and the others joined them.

"Morning," said Lindsey.

"Morning," responded Nathan. "Is this our ride?"

"Do you want the grand tour?" asked Abney.

Badger glared at Cheri and Izumi. "What are you doing? Siding with these motherfuckers?"

"Shut up and listen," snapped Nathan. "This could save your life."

Barnes tapped the taser in his palm to emphasize the point.

The rear emergency exit of the bus had been removed and replaced with a metal ramp. A pair of chains connected to the end of the ramp stretched to the roof and ran through a series of loops welded on either side before disappearing into two holes drilled above the driver's compartment. Abney led them inside. The seats had been removed. Making his way to the front, he stood by the exit stairs and pointed to a metal cage erected around the driver's cab that consisted of dozens of rebar spikes running horizontally and vertically, each welded to one another. The space between each bar was only a few inches. A steel door and frame had been welded into the center. Abney closed the steel door and secured it on the driver's side by dropping a four-foot-long two-by-four into the twin brackets on either side of the mount.

Abney grabbed the cage and shook it as hard as possible. "Once you're in here, nothing will get at you."

Nathan examined the cage. "Looks good, but how do we raise and lower the ramp?"

Abney motioned to the chains dangling from the roof and ending in the cage area. "This is how you control the ramp."

He grabbed the chains and pulled, raising the ramp until it covered the opening in back. A crowbar had been welded to the driver's side of the cage, with the hooked portion pointing down. Abney wrapped the chain several times around the hooked end and secured one of the links through the tip. "When not in use, you secure the chain here."

"Who came up with this?" asked Nathan.

"She did." Abney pointed to Lindsey. "We took the bus that brought us here to White Sands and upgraded it."

"Upgraded it for what?" demanded Badger.

"To catch deaders."

It took a moment for the realization to dawn on him. "No fucking way am I collecting deaders. That's nuts."

"Slade does it," snapped Cheri.

"Yeah, and have you seen the people who do that? They're fucked up."

"You don't have a choice in the matter," said Nathan.

"Yeah, I do. I can refuse to go."

Rizzo stepped forward, a sadistic smile on his face. "We could tase him into unconsciousness and use him as bait."

Nathan pretended to contemplate the suggestion. "That might work."

"Screw you all." Badger tried to back away. Barnes placed

the tip of the taser against his lower back. "Enjoy it while it lasts, assholes. Slade is going to take over this compound and, when he does, the roles will be reversed. Wait till you see the shit I have planned for you."

Cheri stepped forward and slapped Badger off the back of the head.

"What the—?"

"Shut up and listen, dickhead. Slade doesn't give a shit about you or me. He's not going to capture this compound but nuke it out of existence. You'll wind up as a pile of ash. If you help these people out and they stop Slade, you'll live."

"Bullshit," replied Badger, though with less defiance than before.

"It's true." Izumi stepped forward. "I was on the raid to steal a nuclear warhead. He got one and will use it against these people."

"Don't be afraid of what Slade will do to you if you betray him," said Cheri. "You, me, and Izumi are at ground zero. Your only chance of surviving this is if Slade fails."

Nathan placed a hand on Badger's shoulder. "If you cooperate and help us stop Slade, we'll set you free. If not, we'll take you back to the hospital, and you can stay there until this is over."

"Then what happens?"

"You'll get life imprisonment."

Badger studied those around him. Nathan could tell the asshole in him wanted to continue being difficult. Yet he could not deny the obvious. When Badger glanced over at Rizzo, even the guard nodded in a friendly manner.

"Your choice," offered Nathan.

Badger sighed. "What do you want me to do?"

"I'll brief you on the way. You and Cheri are with me. Abney, Lindsey, and Izumi will take point and search for deaders that are easily accessible. The two Bradleys will follow and bail out our asses if we get into trouble. Let's move. I want to be in Alamogordo by sunrise."

Chapter Twenty

THE CONVOY LEFT White Sands via the north gate near Trinity Site, turned right onto Route 380, then headed south along I-54 toward Alamogordo. No one spoke. There was nothing to say. Slade's adventure the other day had riled up the living dead within the city. On the plus side, that would make it easier to round up deaders. On the negative side, they would be more dangerous than ever.

Lindsey took the two-way radio off the dashboard when the convoy reached the intersection where I-54 merged with U.S. Highway I-82. "We're going to scout ahead."

"*Okay,*" responded Nathan. "*Stay safe and good hunting.*"

Abney accelerated. The RAM pulled ahead of the school bus and raced into Alamogordo.

As Nathan watched the pickup pull away, he leaned to the side to speak to Badger and Cheri. "Keep your eyes open for deaders or any other dangers."

"Sure thing." Cheri reached down and placed her hand on the handle of the Glock 23 in its holster.

"How come I don't get a gun?" Badger protested.

"Because I don't trust you enough yet."

"Asshole," he whispered.

"Earn it and I'll give you one."

ABNEY PASSED BENEATH the U.S. Highway 82 overpass and picked up North White Sands Boulevard.

"Do you have any idea where the Scavengers went hunting for deaders?" Abney asked Izumi.

"None. I wasn't briefed on that part of the plan."

Lindsey pointed ahead of her where the road turned left by a Home Depot. A few crushed deaders and fresh tire tracks headed in that direction. "Looks like they went down there."

"Let's give it a shot."

As Abney slowed and made the turn, Lindsey radioed the directions to Nathan. The road curved into a residential neighborhood. A few deaders made their way through the neighborhood in the same direction as the RAM, mostly shamblers and a few that crawled along on fractured legs. One female rotter wearing a tattered, blood-soaked bathrobe teetered on legs with no feet.

"The convoy went this way," said Abney.

"Should we stop?" suggested Lindsey.

Abney shook his head. "Not enough of those things around here to be worth it. Hopefully, we'll find a horde ahead of us."

"Unless Slade's crew already rounded them up," added Izumi.

The neighborhood gave way to open desert and a smaller residential area before turning south. A minute later, Lindsey tapped Abney on the shoulder and pointed ahead of her.

"Jackpot."

Hundreds of deaders milled around the Gerald Chaplain Regional Medical Center.

Abney stopped and shut down the engine so as not to excite the horde, then quietly said to Lindsey, "Let Nathan know we found what he's looking for."

LINDSEY'S VOICE CAME over the radio. *"Are you on North Scenic Drive?"*

Cheri picked up the two-way radio. "Yes. We just turned left onto it at the Home Depot."

"You're going to pass through a residential neighborhood. A mile ahead of you is a horde of deaders near a hospital. We're waiting along the side of the road to help if needed."

"Roger that. See you in a few." Cheri placed the two-way radio back on the dashboard. "You heard that?"

Nathan nodded and glanced over his shoulder at Badger. "Ready?"

"Fuck no. But let's get this over with."

A few minutes later, the hospital came into view, surrounded by the living dead.

"Holy fucking shit," said Badger.

"Are you sure you can handle this?" asked Nathan.

"I don't have much of a choice, do I?"

"If things get out of control, fall back to here."

Nathan drove past the hospital. The twin Bradleys followed, stopping on either side of Abney, and shut down their engines.

As the bus approached, the deaders became agitated.

"We're getting those bastards riled up," said Badger.

Cheri stared at the living dead. "It'll make it easier to get them on the bus."

Nathan accelerated. "Badger, get ready to lure them in."

"Fuck this," he mumbled.

Nathan reached down beside him and gave Badger a baseball bat. "Use this if you have to."

As Badger made his way to the rear of the bus, Nathan raced through the deaders closing in around them. He slammed into nearly a dozen that stumbled into his path, knocking them aside or crushing them beneath the tires. Once ahead of the horde, he stopped the bus and shifted in his seat toward Cheri.

"Lower the ramp."

Cheri removed the links from the curved end of the crowbar. The weight of the ramp yanked them from her hands. The ramp fell open, the edge catching a deader in a hospital security guard's uniform in the head, shattering its skull. The guard collapsed, the corner of the ramp landing on its shoulder. The rest of the horde gathered around, not certain what to do. Others moved against the front and sides of the bus, five of them scratching at the glass doors to get at Cheri.

"What are you waiting for? Lure them in?"

"How?" asked Badger.

"Get down near the ramp and let them see you."

"Fuck that."

"Hurry up or we're going to be swamped."

"Shit." Badger moved down the bus, standing within three feet of the ramp. He banged the bat against the door frame. "Come on, you rotting motherfuckers. I'm right here."

That caught their attention, although they were uncertain where to go.

Badger stepped forward and stomped his foot on the ramp three times. The horde responded to the noise and swarmed around the ramp. Dozens of decaying hands reached out for him. Badger jumped back to avoid their clutch.

"How fucking stupid can you be? I'm right here."

A female deader in a shredded hospital johnnie stumbled over the bottom edge of the ramp and staggered toward the door.

"That's it, bitch. Come and get your Happy Meal."

Noticing the female deader, five others followed.

Badger backed up, keeping a careful eye on the dead. Not looking behind him, he failed to notice the mount for one of the seats that had been removed and tripped over it, falling onto his back. The female deader lunged and landed on top of him. Badger dropped the bat and held up his right arm, his wrist catching its neck and preventing it from biting him. The thing snarled and snapped at the air. With all that weight on his arm, Badger could not hold it back for long.

"I could use some fucking help."

Nathan had already made his way into the back. He yelled

out to Cheri, "Close the ramp."

She grabbed the twin chains as far up as possible and used her body weight to pull them down. The ramp came up halfway, catching two deaders between the metal and the frame, preventing more from entering. However, seven were already in the bus, descending on Badger.

Nathan unholstered his Glock and fired. The first round passed through the neck of the female deader. The second shattered its head. Badger closed his eyes as bits of skull and brain dropped onto his face. The deader's body went limp. Badger tossed it to the side and scrambled to his feet.

Three more grabbed hold of the ramp's edges and tried to pull it down. The added weight made it difficult for Cheri. She leaned back, using all her weight to anchor the chain, but it would not be enough.

"I can only keep it closed for another few seconds."

Badger picked up the bat and stood to Nathan's right. Nathan took down the remaining deaders with well-placed headshots. He placed the Glock on the gore-covered floor and dragged one of the bodies to the side.

"Take care of those trying to get in."

Badger raced to the end of the bus. A male deader with a bloated stomach held on to the right side of the ramp, attempting to pull itself inside. Badger raised the bat and brought it down hard, smashing it in the face. He heard its skull fracture. Part of its head caved in, but the thing kept pulling on the ramp. It glared at Badger and snarled. He struck it again, this time breaking open its head. The bloated deader collapsed, its dead weight falling on the ramp.

The chains tore from Cheri's hands. She screamed as her right index finger got trapped between the links and was nearly torn off. As she watched in horror, the ramp fell open, crushing several deaders beneath it.

A dozen of the living dead ascended.

"SOMETHING'S WRONG," SAID Lindsey as the ramp was raised.

Abney agreed. Concern turned to fear when he heard gunshots coming from inside the bus. He took the two-way off the dashboard.

"Nathan, what's going on?"

No one answered.

Izumi leaned forward between the seats. "We got to do something."

Nathan started the engine and revved it several times. The two Bradleys did the same. The deaders along the outer fringe of the horde staggered toward the rest of the convoy.

Most of the horde remained around the bus, struggling to get inside.

BADGER JUMPED BACK when the ramp fell open.

The living dead surged into the bus.

Nathan had moved the last of the bodies out of the way. He headed for the cab but slipped on the gore, falling to his knees. Frantically searching for his Glock, he could not find it. When he looked up, he knew why.

Badger stood at the entrance to the cab, the weapon in his hands, aimed at Nathan.

"Duck," yelled Badger.

Nathan did. Badger fired three rounds into a female child deader clutching a blood-soaked teddy bear directly behind Nathan. Two tore open its chest. The third struck between its eyes, dropping it.

Badger ran forward and helped Nathan to his feet. As they rushed to the cab, Badger emptied the last three rounds into the closest deaders, buying them the time they needed to escape. Nathan jumped into the driver's seat. Badger slammed shut the cage door and dropped the two-by-four in place as the living dead swarmed the outer side of the cage.

"Thanks," huffed Nathan, trying to catch his breath.

"Don't mention it." Badger handed him the Glock.

"Now what?" asked Cheri.

"We wait until the back is full."

Nathan picked up the two-way radio and keyed the talk button.

IZUMI SWITCHED HER gaze between the two Bradleys. "Why haven't they fired on the deaders?"

"The bus is in the line of—"

Nathan's voice came over the radio. "*Abney, can you hear me?*"

Abney picked it up. "Are you okay?"

"*We had a little trouble here, but things are okay now.*"

"Badger?"

In the background, Badger yelled, "*Screw you.*"

"If it weren't for him, I'd be dead. We'll be ready to roll in a few minutes."

"Roger that."

Abney placed the radio in his lap. Izumi tapped his shoulder and pointed ahead. The pack of deaders was a few yards away.

"Those things are getting close."

"I got this." Abney keyed the talk button on the radio. "Sergeant, do you read me?"

IN THE BRADLEY on the left, Rizzo keyed the talk button. "I read you."

"*See those deaders approaching? Maybe it's time for some target practice.*"

"I was hoping you'd say that."

From inside the turret, Rizzo rotated it toward the pack and aimed the 25mm M242 Bushmaster chain gun. The Bushmaster shredded them, blasting away chunks of the living dead. Rizzo walked the barrel along the length of the pack, leaving a trail of human detritus in its path. A mist of congealed blood and gore formed around them. It took less than thirty seconds to clear the area. When Rizzo removed his finger from the trigger, nothing remained but a killing field of the living dead.

Someone tugged on Rizzo's pants leg. He looked down. A corporal waved the radio.

"Nathan says thanks."

"Tell him it was the most fun I've had in months."

BADGER KEPT SWITCHING his position to get a better look at the rear of the bus until he could finally see the ramp.

"We're full."

"Then let's get out of here."

Nathan shifted into drive and accelerated. The bus moved forward a few feet and then stopped. He attempted it a second time with the same results. Shifting into reverse, he tried backing up, but the ramp ground against the asphalt. Nathan shifted into drive again. This time the bus moved forward an extra foot or two before stopping.

Cheri became frightened. "What's wrong?"

"There's too many deaders in front. I can't push through them."

"Back up and get some running speed," suggested Badger.

"The ramp is down. We could damage the bus and then be stuck here."

Badger looked over his shoulder and noticed the Challenger and the two Bradleys backing up. He took the two-way radio from Nathan and keyed the talk button.

"Hey, assholes in the armored cars. We're surrounded by these fuckers and can't move. How about doing your job and clearing some of them out?"

Rizzo responded. "*Is Nathan hurt?*"

Badger stared at the radio. "Why do you ask?"

"*He's in charge.*"

The deaders pounding on the side door to the bus finally shattered the narrow window. Glass showered the cab floor, followed by dead hands reaching in. Cheri cried out and moved out of their reach.

Nathan leaned over and shouted into the speaker, "Hurry up and get us out of here."

"*Roger that.*"

RIZZO KEYED HIS intercom to speak to the driver of their Bradley. "Connors, did you get that?"

"I did, Sarge."

"Move up along their left flank and clear those things away. I'll take care of the ones in front. Tucker, stay here and be ready to push Nathan if he needs it."

"*Loud and clear,*" responded the driver of the second Bradley.

"Then let's do this."

IZUMI GASPED WHEN the Bradley lurched forward. "What's going on?"

Abney looked over his shoulder at her. "Hang on. This is where it gets exciting."

NATHAN HANDED BADGER the Glock and a spare magazine. As Badger reloaded, Cheri picked up the baseball bat and, holding it in the center and by the handle, rammed it into the face of a female nurse in hospital scrubs with baby ducks and chicks on it. Each blow crushed in its face bones or shattered rotten teeth. When Badger finished switching out magazines, he moved in front of Cheri and placed a bullet between the nurse deader's eyes. The body collapsed and went limp. Its arm caught in the broken window, leaving the deader dangling on the door and preventing others from filling the gap.

Nathan spotted movement in his side mirror as the Bradley approached.

"Hang on. This could get bumpy."

CONNORS MANEUVERED THE Bradley alongside the bus, careful to leave only a few inches between the two vehicles. Those deaders not crushed under the armored car's tires were ground together and torn apart between the two vehicles. The snarling grew more intensive, generating a death knell that sent a shiver down Rizzo's spine. As horrifying as the sound was, it failed to compare to the overwhelming stench of decayed bodies being churned apart and the swarm of insects that swarmed around the turret's viewfinder.

Once the Bradley passed the front fender of the bus, Rizzo spun the turret to the right and opened fire on the swarm in front of the vehicle. Bodies blew apart. Chunks of decayed flesh and severed limbs mixed with congealed blood and liquified organs, covering the road and splattering the bus's windshield. Only a pile of gore remained when Connors veered slightly to the left to open a path.

NATHAN WAITED UNTIL the Bradley was clear before accelerating. The bus moved forward several yards before slowing, its back end swerving to the left. He heard the sound of spinning rubber as the rear tires struggled to get a grip on the road.

"Fucking great," said Badger.

Nathan agreed but did not have time to complain. He shifted into neutral and took his foot off the gas pedal. The bus slid back a yard. Nathan accelerated again, this time turning the steering wheel to the right. The change in direction allowed the right rear tires to touch clear ground. The bus lurched forward, knocking Badger and Cheri off balance, and headed up the road. Those deaders that had survived stumbled along after it.

Abney and the second Bradley fell in behind them.

When the deaders climbing the ramp fell off, Badger and Cheri grabbed the chains and pulled, raising the ramp until it closed over the exit, then secured the chains on the crowbars.

Nathan keyed the radio. "Sergeant, thanks for the assist."

"*That's what I'm here for. What now?*"

"We head back to White Sands, drop off this bunch, and return to get more."

"You gotta be fucking kidding?" blurted Badger.

"I wish. We have to do this several times a day until Slade attacks the compound."

"Fuck my luck."

Chapter Twenty-One

S LADE MADE HIS rounds of the Vesta compound, ostensibly
to raise morale before the attack on White Sand. In
reality, he needed to occupy himself. The operation was
planned, and the teams were making the final preparations,
leaving him with nothing to do. He also wanted to get away
from Gina for a while. She had become bitchy the past few
days, arguing with him over the necessity to destroy the
community at White Sands rather than taking them over or,
even better, convincing President Martinetti to join their cause.
Slade had already decided to send her to Big Jake's after those
in the back room had been cleared out.

First, he checked with Vince. The sixty-three followers of
Reverend Moon brought back to Vesta had all reanimated by
this morning as well as the member of Vince's team accidentally bitten. Adding the twelve women from Big Jake's and the
nine sitting in jail brought the number of suicide deaders to
eighty-five. Not quite the one hundred he had wanted, but still
enough to blow a path through White Sand's defenses and get
the warhead into their compound.

Assuming they had a working device. Zach had sung his
own praise on how he could override the warhead's built-in
triggering device and replace it with one of his design. That
bravado faded after the little shit realized what he had gotten
himself into. Worst case scenario, they could use the warhead
as a dirty bomb. Rather than implode the core and generate a
nuclear reaction, they could explode the casing and warhead,

strewing radioactive material across the compound. No mass destruction would devastate the area, but Martinetti would have to move her people elsewhere or let them die from radiation poisoning. Once on the road, they would be vulnerable to his Scavengers.

Slade would not let Zach know that. The kid's numerous successes had gone to his head to the point that, at Kirtland, Zach challenged his decisions. The kid needed to be brought back in line. Slade would never throw him in with the suicide deaders, but he had no problem doing so with Tara. She meant nothing to him or the safety of Vesta. Hopefully, doing that would scare the shit out of the little ass—

"Boss." Candolini rushed up. "I've been looking for you."

Slade frowned. Everyone came to him with problems rather than fixing it themselves.

"What is it this time?"

Candolini ignored the Boss' irritation. "We've been trying to reach you for half an hour."

"I left the radio in my quarters. I wanted a few minutes without being bothered."

"The geek wants to see you."

Slade's eyes narrowed. "Did he say why?"

"No. He just said it was important."

"Thanks."

Candolini nodded and walked away. Slade sighed. There went his peaceful afternoon.

Making his way to the lab, Slade entered without knocking, hoping to catch them off guard. He expected Zach to be apologetic and contrite. Instead, he and Tara were in a good mood and excited.

"I hope I'm not here so you can tell me the device won't work."

"No need to worry." Zach stepped over to the warhead and motioned for Slade to join him. "I removed the barometric triggering mechanism and replaced it with this."

The kid pointed to a metal device the size and shape of a cigar box on the workbench. An unlit LED display was built into it. An L-shaped antenna five inches long extended from the right side. Beside the device was something that looked like a joystick for vintage video games, orange in color and with an extendable antenna on top. A red button was on the back of the joystick where the thumb would sit. A covered toggle switch sat opposite the button on the front. A pair of darkened green lights the size of dimes sat above the red button.

"What's this?"

Zach picked up the device with the LED display. "This will initiate the explosion. I can set it either for a timed or immediate detonation." Holding the device in his left hand, he picked up the joystick and handed it to Slade. "This initiates the process. Press the red button."

Slade complied. The light above and to the left glowed green. On the device, the LED display lit up. The number three appeared. A red light above the LED came on.

"The detonator is primed. Now, flip up the cover on the front."

Slade did. Beneath it was a toggle switch in the up position.

"Push it down."

Slade stared at him with an expression of uncertainty.

"Don't worry. It won't work unless it's attached to the warhead."

Taking a deep breath, Slade toggled the switch into the down position. The green light to the right of the first came on. On the timer, a green light above the LED came on. The numbers on the LED counted down from three. When it displayed zero, an electronic click came from inside the timer.

"Your warhead just went off."

"How long can the timer be set for?"

"Anywhere from several hours to an instant detonation. This morning, I had one of the drivers take me out with the trigger while Tara stayed here with the detonator. We tested it under various scenarios. The effective range is ten miles, which provides a decent safe zone from which to set it off."

Slade nodded. "Impressive. I knew you could do it."

"And that's not all." Zach gestured toward Tara.

She smiled and led Slade over to another workbench. Fifty-seven neck bombs sat arranged in six rows of six, with one off to the side.

"What are these for? We've already armed the suicide deaders."

"We were low on supplies," interceded Zach. "We used them up and made as many as possible. That's it until we go on another scavenger run."

"Hopefully, we won't need any more. Once White Sands is gone, we'll be the strongest force in the southwest. If the others are smart, they'll fall in line."

"And if they don't?"

"Then they'll wish they had." Slade no longer wanted to continue this conversation. "How long will it take to mount the detonator onto the warhead."

"Ten minutes, fifteen at most. For safety reasons, I won't attach it until we're on the road and far away from Vesta."

"Fair enough. You both did a great job here. You should be proud of yourselves. Take the night off and go to Big Jake's. The drinks are on the house."

"Thank you, but I don't—"

"We'll be there." Tara slipped both arms around Zach's right and squeezed.

Slade suppressed a smile and left, returning to his quarters. He would have Candolini check with the motor pool and Vince's team, getting an estimate of how long it will take them to be ready. Once they were prepared, he could finally take out White Sand and rule the southwest.

Chapter Twenty-Two

"HOW DO YOU feel today?" asked Roni as she stepped beside Mr. Spritzer's bed.

"Pretty good." The old man forced a smile. It became genuine when he saw Alissa on the other side of the bed. "I must have died and gone to Heaven because I see an angel."

Alissa stroked his hair. "You say that all the time."

"Because it's true."

"Calm down. You'll raise your blood pressure." Roni ran the thermometer/pulse oximeter across his scalp. "Your pulse is eighty-eight, and your temperature is 97.8. Not bad. How do you feel?"

"It doesn't hurt as much as I thought it would."

"That's because of the morphine." Roni withdrew a blood pressure machine from her pocket, wrapped the cuff around his upper right arm, and then pressed the electronic device's start button. "We'll keep giving that to you until the pain from the surgery dies down."

"Will I get addicted?"

"No."

"Damn," Mr. Spritzer replied with mock disappointment.

Alissa patted his hand. "You don't want to be high all the time, do you?"

"Considering what's going on out there, why not?"

"But then you wouldn't be able to flirt with me."

"That's true. And you being here makes me happy already."

"Oh, God." Roni chuckled and shook her head. When the machine had finished its readings, she loosened the cuff and removed it. "One hundred thirty-four over seventy-two. You're recovering nicely. Is everything else okay?"

"What's odd is my leg itches."

"That's natural." Roni placed a hand on his shoulder. "O'Brien will be by in an hour with lunch. You rest until then."

Mr. Spritzer gave her a thumbs up, then wiggled his fingers at Alissa in a wave.

The two ladies stepped out into the hall.

"He seems to be doing well," said Alissa.

"He'll recover."

"Will you be able to get him a prosthetic?"

"Eventually, yes. Finding one to fit him properly will be hard, but O'Brien can jury-rig it. Until then, I have a wheel-chair at the clinic he can—"

The two-way radio in the pocket of her lab coat squawked. O'Brien's voice came through the speaker, a tinge of fear in his tone.

"*Roni, are you there?*"

Roni pressed the talk button. "I'm here. What's wrong?"

"*You need to meet me where the road meets the top of the mesa.*"

"Why don't you tell me over—"

"*Quickly,*" he said forcefully.

"Be right there." She slid the radio back into her pocket and headed for the front door, waving for Alissa to follow.

THEY DROVE THE ATV to the northern edge of the mesa where the two-lane road descended into the desert. O'Brien had parked the Sierra so it partially blocked the road. He stood behind the bed, a pair of binoculars focused on the horizon. Roni parked alongside the pickup, and the two women joined him.

"What's wrong?" asked Roni.

"That." O'Brien handed her the binoculars and pointed north.

Roni studied the horizon briefly before mumbling, "Shit."

"What's wrong?" asked Alissa, concerned that whatever was out there had shaken Roni.

"See for yourself." She handed Alissa the binoculars.

Alissa scanned the horizon and immediately thought Roni's response was an understatement.

A horde of deaders approached. At this distance, there were too many to count, but she estimated at least three to four hundred.

"They're following the road straight to here," said O'Brien. "I estimate they'll be here in over an hour."

Roni thought for a moment. "Our best bet is to block the road. Hopefully, they'll go around the mesa."

"I'd be careful if you try that," advised Alissa.

"Why?"

Alissa handed Roni the binoculars. "Check out the way they walk. They're strolling rather than staggering."

"What does that mean?" asked O'Brien.

"It means they're runners. If we excite them, they'll charge this place."

Roni studied the horde before mumbling, "Double shit."

"What do you have for defense?" asked Alissa.

"Just a few weapons and some tools."

"That's not enough to hold them off."

"What should we do?" asked O'Brien.

Roni started to reply but paused. Alissa realized the woman knew how to help the living but had no idea how to deal with the dead. She would have to take charge.

She turned to O'Brien. "Where's the truck we used to get the supplies from the vet store?"

"Back at the clinic."

"Park it across the road at the bottom of the mesa. And haul ass."

"Why?"

"Once those things hear the truck, they'll charge it. You need to be well away from there when that happens."

O'Brien did not need to be told twice. He jumped into the Sierra and sped back to the clinic.

Alissa climbed behind the steering wheel of the ATV and waved for Roni to join her. "Come on."

"Where are we going?"

"To get the diesel tanker."

Chapter Twenty-Three

O'BRIEN DROVE SO fast that the Sierra swerved around the corner to the rear of the clinic. He slammed on the brakes, creating a cloud of dust as the pickup slid to a stop alongside the Ryder. In his excitement, he forgot to shift into Park. As he opened the door and started to get out, the pickup rolled forward. O'Brien lost balance and almost fell out of the cab, twisting his left ankle under the chassis. A bolt of pain shot up his leg. Reaching back in, he applied the emergency brakes and shifted into neutral. His left leg almost gave out the minute he applied pressure to it. Thankfully, nothing was broken, only badly bruised.

O'Brien limped over to the Ryder, climbed in, started the engine, and proceeded back to the road.

ALISSA SWERVED TO avoid hitting the Ryder, nearly tipping the ATV onto its side. She swung around to the rear of the clinic and stopped in front of the diesel tanker. "Are the keys inside?"

"They're either in the ignition or the visor."

"Good." Alissa jumped out and paused. "Go back to the house and get anything that can be used as a weapon. Give them to Chris and have him meet me back at the road. You stay with the patients."

Roni slid over into the driver's seat and shifted into drive. "Good luck."

As Roni raced uphill to the house, Alissa climbed into the cab of the diesel tanker and started the engine. Only then did she realize the truck was a standard. The last time she had driven one was in junior high when her boyfriend taught her how to drive with a shift. She had to learn again, only now on a truck.

Alissa placed her left foot on the clutch, shifted into drive, and shifted from the clutch to the gas pedal. The truck lurched forward and stalled. Alissa swore under her breath and tried again. The truck made it a few feet before stalling. Taking a deep breath, she tried a third time. The engine sputtered and threatened to stall. Alissa pressed her foot harder on the pedal. The tanker accelerated without stalling.

She followed the Ryder.

RONI PARKED THE ATV in front of her house and ran inside, heading for the stairs.

"Is everything okay?" yelled Mr. Spritzer from his room.

"Yes. Stay calm. I'll be back in a minute."

"If everything's okay, why do I need to stay calm?"

Roni did not listen, racing upstairs to the room where Chris recovered. She barged in without knocking, startling him out of a nap.

"You scared the shit out of me."

"You should be scared." Roni rushed over to the chair where his clothes lay in a folded pile, grabbed them, and tossed them onto the bed. "We have several hundred runners heading this way."

Chris swung his legs out of bed and stripped out of his pajamas. "Where's Alissa?"

"She and O'Brien are preparing a barricade at the bottom of the mesa. She told me to gather up every weapon I had and give them to you. You'll meet her where the road meets the top of the mesa." She paused at the door. "I'll be in the kitchen when you're done."

It took Chris less than two minutes to get dressed despite the aching of his muscles and the dull throb in his head. By the time he made it downstairs to the kitchen, Roni had laid out everything she had that could serve as a weapon—the .308 Winchester bolt-action hunting rifle with a scope, the Mossberg 12-gauge pump action shotgun, the 9mm Makarov, two axes, three crowbars, a pick, and a shovel.

"Any other firearms?"

"Just these."

"Do you have spare ammo?"

"Just a second." Roni ran out of the room.

Chris put aside the rifle, shotgun, axes, and crowbars.

Roni returned a minute later with three boxes of shotgun shells and one box of rifle rounds. "Here."

"Thanks." He slid the boxes into his pants pockets and handed the Makarov to Roni. "Take this."

"I'll never be able to defend the house with this."

"It's not for defense. It's in case we fail."

"I don't under…." It suddenly dawned on Roni what he meant. "Dear God, please don't fail."

"I don't intend to. How do I get to Alissa and O'Brien?"

"There's an ATV out front. The keys are in the ignition. Follow the driveway to the main road and turn right. It's less than a mile from here."

"Lock the door behind me and make certain the windows are secure."

"Of course."

Chris picked up the weapons and headed for the front door. Roni opened it for him, then closed and locked it behind him. He placed the weapons on the back seat, jumped behind the wheel, and headed out.

O'BRIEN REACHED THE top of the mesa road and stopped to

check out the situation. The horde had approached to within a mile. This would be close.

He shifted into neutral and coasted down the road, making as little noise as possible. It worked. The horde still shambled along. At the bottom, he applied the brakes, veered to the left, stopped at an angle, and started the engine. The sound caught the horde's attention. The living dead broke into a run, heading straight for the Ryder.

O'Brien shifted into reverse and turned the steering wheel, backing the rear of the truck against the walls of the pass, then shifted back into drive, turned the wheel to the left, and pulled forward a few feet. He repeated the process until he had wedged the truck into the opening, leaving no room for the deaders to get—

The passenger side window shattered, covering him in shards of glass. A large deader in a National Guard uniform reached into the cab, growling and frantically clutching at O'Brien. The rest of the horde slammed into the truck, their weight tilting it to one side. As the deaders in the back crawled on top of the others, the slant increased until it became top-heavy and rolled over. O'Brien slid against the driver's door, bracing himself. The truck finally came to rest at a forty-five-degree angle when the roof of the Ryder caught against the wall of the pass.

His relief was short-lived. With the cab resting at an angle, the National Guard deader crawled further through the window. It would have fallen into the cab if the mass of deaders pushing against the outside had not pinned its legs. The thing hovered a few feet above O'Brien, congealed blood and maggot-filled pieces of rotting flesh dripping from its mouth. Outside, an increasing number of the living dead climbed up the undercarriage. They would overwhelm him within seconds.

Bracing his back against the door, O'Brien slammed the heel of his boot against the National Guard deader's face. Each blow ripped off chunks of flesh. The third and fourth shattered most of its front teeth. The sixth dislodged its lower jaw, which dangled from a strip of flesh on the right side of its face. Despite its injuries, it continued its attack—

A gunshot broke through the moans of the living dead. The windshield shattered and the head of the National Guard deader erupted, spewing detritus across O'Brien's face. As he wiped it off, a hand grabbed his collar. O'Brien fought back, blindly punching in the direction of his attacker.

"Knock it off. It's me, Chris. I'm getting you out of here."

"Hurry."

A second deader, this one a teenage girl with both hands chewed off, crawled over the body of the National Guard deader, dragging itself into the cab. Chris aimed the shotgun at its head and fired, blasting away the top of its skull. The body went limp, dropping more gore on O'Brien. As Chris picked off any deader making it over the top of the truck, O'Brien pulled himself up from the driver's seat and climbed through the shattered windshield, losing his grip and falling onto the asphalt.

"Shit."

"Are you okay?" asked Chris.

"Yeah. Just bruised my shoulder."

Chris helped O'Brien to his feet, and the two raced over to the ATV parked fifty feet from the truck.

ALISSA WATCHED FROM the top of the mesa as Chris rescued O'Brien. They had arrived only a few minutes ago in time to see the runners swarm and tip over the Ryder. Chris gave Alissa the Winchester and raced down the road. She stood guard, ready to pick off any of the living dead that got past the barricade. None did until after Chris and O'Brien jumped back into the ATV.

One deader climbed up onto the right fender of the truck. On seeing the ATV, it crouched and snarled. Alissa lined up the scope's crosshairs with its head, held her breath, and slowly squeezed the trigger. The bullet struck the deader in the right shoulder, knocking it off balance. It looked around for its attacker. Alissa lined up her shot and fired. This time the round struck the temple, blowing off the left side of its head. It tumbled backward off the truck. A second deader took its place.

A deader in a security guard uniform realized that a large space existed beneath the Ryder. Dropping to its knees, the thing crawled under the chassis and jumped to its feet. Alissa fired a round that struck it in the chest. The second hit to the right of its nose, shattering the upper jaw and tearing through the primordial brain. It staggered for a second before collapsing.

The damage had been done. Other deaders had seen the security guard crawl under the truck and followed. Within seconds, thirty-two runners had gone under and were racing up the road, too many for Alissa to take down. More followed.

Chris pulled the ATV beside Alissa.

"How much ammo do we have?" she asked.

Chris took the Winchester and gave Alissa the shotgun and three boxes of rounds.

"That's not enough to stop them," said O'Brien.

"Which is why I brought that." Alissa pointed over her shoulder to the diesel tanker.

She shouldered the shotgun and led O'Brien to the bucket box at the end of the truck. O'Brien opened it, revealing the hose, reel, and meters. Unwinding the hose, he dragged it over to where the road began its decline and placed it on the ground with the nozzle facing down, then stepped back against the truck.

"Stand clear."

Alissa moved out of the way. O'Brien flipped a switch. The pump stiffened and, a moment later, a stream of diesel fuel spewed from the nozzle, splashing against the asphalt and flowing down the road.

The closest deader, a little girl with its left arm missing and clutching a gore-covered teddy bear in its right, had made it halfway up the road. Chris took out the girl deader with a single headshot, then switched to those in the rear.

"How much fuel should we use?" asked O'Brien.

"The flow has to reach the truck where most of the horde is." Judging by how many deaders had made it past the barricade and how fast they were nearing the top of the mesa, she doubted they could wait that long.

An increasing number of deaders slipped under the truck and made their way up the road. Chris took out those farthest away while Alissa waited for the closest to draw near before blasting them down.

The diesel fuel finally reached the truck. Small pools formed around the wheels and overflowed, flowing past the undercarriage.

"Let's do this."

O'Brien closed the spigot. "I need to move the tanker out of the way."

"Do you have anything to ignite it?" asked Alissa.

"There are flares in the ATV."

As O'Brien pulled the tanker ten feet forward, Alissa rushed over to the ATV and searched for the flares, finding them in the compartment behind the seats.

A male deader naked from the waist up, its abdomen torn open and its insides missing, lunged at her. Close behind it was a female deader, half of its face eaten away. Alissa aimed and fired. The head of the male deader exploded. The next round tore into the chest of the female deader, creating a mist of congealed blood and gore but barely slowing it. The third round blasted away its face.

"Hurry!"

"Got it." Alissa raced over, lit the flare, and tossed it.

The fuel ignited with a thunderous swoosh. A wall of fire

sprung up and rapidly surged down the road, engulfing the scores of deaders racing to the top. None made a sound as the flames consumed them. It reached the truck and spread around the vehicle. Flames crept up the cargo bay and the cab. A few seconds later, the fuel tanks ignited, dousing the remaining horde gathered behind it.

The runners halfway up the road collapsed as their leg muscles shriveled and burned, their bodies dropping into the melting asphalt and writhing around until consumed by the inferno. Those already near the top kept advancing, their limbs on fire. Alissa and Chris picked them off one by one. They both ran out of ammo at the same time and paused to reload.

A snarl caught Alissa's attention. A flaming deader was ten feet away. She only had time to raise the shotgun and slam the stock into its face, sending up a cloud of embers. One fell on her good eye, momentarily blinding her. Closing her lid, she jammed the shotgun at the deader, feeling the impact of the stock against its face. A flaming hand grabbed her collar. Alissa felt the fire singing her skin.

"Hold still," yelled O'Brien.

Alissa opened her eye in time to see O'Brien charging, the crowbar raised above his head. He brought it down on top of the deader's skull. The metal tip shattered the bone and embedded in the thing's brain. It convulsed and released its grip. Alissa jumped back and patted out the fire on her shirt. O'Brien whipped the crowbar to the side, toppling over the deader. It lay on the ground, crackling as the flames consumed it. The stench of burning decayed flesh filled the air.

O'Brien dropped to his knees and vomited.

Chris ran over and hugged Alissa. "Are you okay?"

"I'm fine."

"You were burned."

"Not badly. It'll heal."

"Is the baby okay?"

"Yes." Alissa leaned forward and kissed Chris. "We'll all be fine now."

O'Brien got back to his feet and wiped the vomitus off his mouth.

"How are you doing?" asked Chris.

"Embarrassed. I've never been this close to burning dead-ers before."

"We have." Alissa smiled.

"Are you serious?"

Both she and Chris nodded and grinned. They had been through a lot together.

O'Brien pointed to the Ryder at the bottom of the mesa. "That's going to be one hell of a mess to clean up."

Below them, flames engulfed the truck, charring the metal black. A huge pile of living dead surrounded the vehicle, some still thrashing about. Other charred bodies littered the road.

It would be a nightmare to clean up, thought Alissa. *But at least they were still alive to do it.*

Chapter Twenty-Four

A N AIR OF uncertainty hung over President Martinetti as she drove into the desert to watch the sunrise. The Scavenger attack on White Sands was inevitable, the only variables being when it would take place and how Slade would carry it out. Though nobody would state it publicly, everyone knew the odds were stacked against them. It bothered Martinetti more than the others since she was responsible for the compound's safety.

She turned off the main road heading north and proceeded farther into the desert. After a few miles, the president arrived at a location surrounded by two chain-link fences. Parking by the outer one, she climbed out of the cart and walked through the barbed wire corridor connecting the exterior and interior gates. Ahead of her sat a twelve-foot-high obelisk constructed out of black lava. On the side facing the gates, barely visible in the pre-dawn light illuminating the eastern horizon, a metal plague had been mounted that read:

TRINITY SITE
WHERE
THE WORLD'S FIRST
NUCLEAR DEVICE
WAS EXPLODED ON
JULY 16, 1945

How ironic, thought Martinetti. *It might also be the location of the last device exploded.*

Martinetti chastised herself for thinking that way. Her people had done everything possible to ensure they could deal with whatever Slade threw at them. Carrington already had produced enough of the anti-virus serum to cure several hundred people who might be bitten, significantly increasing the odds of surviving a deader onslaught. According to Colonel Roberts, trenches had been dug around twenty percent of the compound, and the deaders captured over the last few days had been prepared for use against the Scavengers. Those numbers would increase each day until the attack took place. As of this morning, lookouts would be posted along the routes leading from Vesta to White Sands to give them advance warning of an impending attack, which had helped them to thwart the one against Alamogordo a few days ago.

Only this time, there would be two significant differences.

First, Slade would be launching a direct assault against White Sands rather than a diversionary skirmish to cover the main operation at Kirtland.

Second, this time Slade would have a nuclear weapon at his disposal.

The sun's rays crested the Oscura Mountains and moved slowly across the desert. A surprised rabbit bolted across the sand and darted into its burrow. A lizard perched on the side of the obelisk spun around when it felt the sun's warmth and scurried down to its lair beneath the monument. Behind her, a flock of Sandhill Cranes took off into flight, passing over Martinetti's head before flying west.

As the light washed across the plaque, Martinetti reread it. The realization dawned on her. Over a quarter of a century after the first nuclear device was detonated here, life flourished around this spot again. And the day still dawned, providing the comfort of light following the fear of darkness. It was irrelevant whether they defeated Slade or he emerged the winner. It mattered little whether Slade detonated the warhead. Whatever the outcome of the next several days, one fact remained certain.

Good eventually emerges the victor.

"IT'S SO GOOD to see you're doing better," said Nathan.

"I'm glad to be out of the infirmary." Fifty-Fifty used his good arm to sip at his coffee. "The doc said I can be released for a few hours a day as long as I don't use it."

The kid had joined him, Abney, and Lindsey that morning in the mess hall for breakfast. Nathan could not help but notice they were the only members of the group still mobile and able to function. What a shit show they had gotten themselves into.

"How are Tupoc and Liam?" asked Abney.

The kid's enthusiasm lessened. "As good as can be expected. Tupoc will never get back full use of his hands, and Liam will be scarred for life. He's driving the staff nuts."

"Why?" asked Nathan.

"He keeps complaining to the doctors and nurses that he belongs out here helping us get ready for the next attack."

"What do they tell him?"

"That he's suffered burns that won't heal unless he takes care of himself. Liam keeps arguing that he doesn't plan on slapping deaders with his face."

Lindsey laughed, spitting out her coffee. Abney sighed.

"That sounds like Liam."

Fifty-Fifty took another drink. "Listening to him complain all day is the main reason I want to get out of there for a few hours."

"I can arrange to get him out and help around here," offered Nathan. "We can find something for him to do that won't aggravate his injuries. And it'll free up someone for the front lines."

"Thanks." Fifty-Fifty nodded his gratitude. "He'll appreciate it."

Lindsey smiled. "I have a feeling the hospital staff will appreciate it even more."

The group enjoyed a chuckle.

"How's Malcolm?" Nathan asked.

Lindsey sighed and Abney rolled his eyes.

"What?"

Nathan answered. "He blames himself for us not stopping Slade at Kirtland and has been trying to make up for it since."

"It wasn't his fault. Slade's people ambushed us."

"We know," agreed Lindsey. "But try telling him that. He's been busting his ass to stop Slade from succeeding during his next attack. Kiera has been helping him the past few days. Earlier this morning, she made him take a few sleeping pills to get some rest."

"God knows he needed it," added Abney.

An uncomfortable silence ensued until Fifty-Fifty asked the question everyone else avoided.

"Do we know when and how the Scavengers will attack?"

"Not a clue," answered Nathan.

"Did he get the nuke? Does it work?"

Nathan shrugged. "Malcolm is certain they stole at least one, but whether his people can get it to work is another thing. We're hoping for the best."

"And planning for the worst," added Abney. Lindsey reached out and held his hand.

Fifty-Fifty looked concerned. "What are our chances of stopping Slade?"

Nathan, Abney, and Lindsey exchanged glances, no one wanting to admit the truth. Finally, Lindsey answered.

"Our chances of coming through this are not good."

KIERA CROSSED THE compound, struggling to stay awake. She and Malcolm had been working on less than four hours of sleep a night since returning to White Sands. He had been able to keep going on a combination of guilt and anxiety and, to his credit, had not only figured out the code to detonate the neck bombs but came up with new defenses for the compound. Kiera only wished she had the same level of energy. Far from it. That was why she convinced Malcolm to take sleeping pills and get some much-needed rest. While he slept, she went back to her quarters for a long sleep.

And to see her family, maybe for the last time.

Kiera entered her room, happy to see her mother had not yet left for her shift. Little Stevie sat on the floor playing with Archer and Thor. The puppy kept getting excited around Archer and ran over to play, jumping around and nipping playfully at the cat's face. When Archer finally had enough, he would stand on his hind legs, hiss at the puppy, and smack him several times in the head. Thor would yelp and race away, only to come back for more a few seconds later.

"Hello."

Miriam looked up. On seeing her daughter, she beamed with delight. She jumped up, ran over, and embraced Kiera.

"I'm so glad to see you." Miriam refused to let go.

"Me, too." Kiera held her mother longer than she usually did.

When they finally broke their embrace, the two women sat on the edge of a bunk, holding hands. Little Stevie waved at Kiera and continued playing with the pets.

"They remind me of me and Stevie," she said.

"How so?" asked Miriam.

"An older sibling being annoyed by the younger, immature one."

"That's not nice," chuckled Miriam.

Little Stevie stopped petting Archer long enough to raise his right hand and extend the middle finger.

"You be nice to each other."

"We are being nice," said Kiera.

Little Stevie smiled. "You should see us when we're mean."

Miriam smiled, placed her arm around Kiera's arm, and pulled her close. Kiera placed her head on her mother's shoulder.

SLADE AND CANDOLINI sat across from each in the Boss' office as Candolini briefed him on the progress the teams had made finalizing the preparations for the attack on White Sands. The news was all positive, which made Slade happy. Soon he would have his revenge for the failed attack several weeks ago on the convoy from St. Louis, the one that injured his leg. He waited until Candolini concluded before asking his question.

"How many people do we have as reserves?"

"Fifty."

"How well are they trained?'

"They received the basics. They know how to fire a weapon and were taught rudimentary fighting skills. A few of them have been outside the compound once or twice. None have fired a weapon since training."

"Add them to the operation."

Candolini raised an eyebrow. "Are you sure? They might be more of a hindrance."

"I don't plan to put them on the front line. They can stay to the rear and free up the experienced Scavengers for the fight. We'll only use them if necessary."

"Whatever you say."

"Give them half a day of training on weapons to sharpen their skills. It'll make them more confident going into combat."

"Roger that. Do we have a set date to launch this operation?"

"What day is today?"

Candolini shrugged. "I haven't looked at a calendar since this shit began."

"Me neither. We'll set out at 0300 three days from now."

"I'll let the other teams know. Is there anything else?"

"Just one more thing." Slade opened the bottom drawer of his desk and removed a half-empty bottle of Maker's Mark whiskey and two tumblers, which he placed on the desktop.

"I didn't think you drank."

"Usually, I don't." Slade unscrewed the cap, poured an inch of whiskey into each glass, and then slid one across to his second. "But this is a special occasion."

"I won't argue." Candolini held the tumbler in front of him. "Here's to the success of the operation."

Slade added, "And taking out White Sands once and for all."

"YOU'VE BEEN STARING at that warhead for hours." Tara lightly massaged Zach's shoulders.

Zach's interest in science began when he was ten and watched a re-run of *The Day After* about a nuclear war and how survivors in the mid-West tried to rebuild society. Zach spent the next week online reading everything he could download on nuclear weapons, from their creation during World War II up to the end of the Cold War and their development by rogue states like Iraq and North Korea. As time passed, his interests branched out into more useful fields like engineering. Still, he always maintained a deep fascination for nuclear weapons and planned on joining the Air Force to work with them. He had always wanted to see an operative weapon up close.

Now that his dream had come true, Zach wished he had never been fascinated by science and instead obsessed over sports and girls.

When he did not answer, Tara leaned closer and hugged him from behind. "Come on. Let's go to bed."

Zach took her right hand and kissed it. "Please don't take

this the wrong way, but I'm not in the mood."

"Then let's go for a walk. Anything that gets you out of this lab and your mind off that thing for a while."

"It won't work." Zach's voice dripped with despair. "Did you know nuclear weapons have only been used against humans twice?"

"Yeah. Those two cities in Japan at the end of the Second World War."

Zach nodded. "In a few days, the third time will take place at White Sands. Because of me. And it won't be to end a war but to give Slade power."

"There's nothing you could have done."

Anger flared inside Zach, not at Tara but himself. "I could have refused to go along."

"Then you would have wound up as a suicide deader, and Slade would have found someone else to do it."

"I doubt anyone else could."

Tara sighed. She moved around in front of Zach and crouched, making eye contact.

"The Americans dropped those bombs on Japan to end the war and save lives. You're doing the same thing."

"It's not the same."

"It is." Tara took his hands and squeezed. "Slade will stop at nothing to rule the area. How many convoys from St. Louis has he ambushed? He took over that religious compound in Colorado and turned those people into suicide deaders. Shit, he did that to our people."

"You're kidding?"

"Slade cleaned out the prison and the girls in Big Jake's back room. I was friends with some of them. Think about it. If he hadn't taken me out and… I'd be a suicide deader myself."

"But it's wrong to use a nuke against White Sands."

"It's not a question of right or wrong." Tara spoke firmly to make her point. "It's a question of survival. Am I happy that he's sacrificing his own people? No. But be honest. Do you think those people in White Sands are better than those living here? Are their lives any more valuable than yours? Or mine? Of course not. All I want is for us to survive this shit and get on with our lives."

Zach sat up straight. "Our lives?"

Tara smiled. "Face it, kid. You're stuck with me."

Tara was right. They both had something to live for—each other.

Zach stood and clasped her hand. "Come on. That walk sounds good."

MONICA ARRIVED AT the warehouse early the next morning. Not because she was anxious to get to work. Screw that. She had the worst hangover of her life. Since lying in her bunk did no good, she decided to take a walk, hoping the fresh air might help. It did not.

Last night, the team had overdone it at Big Jake's after turning those in jail and those consigned to the bar's back room into suicide deaders. It had been disturbing enough murdering and turning Reverend Moon's followers, but these were their own people. Shit, it could as easily have been one of them. When she first arrived at Vesta, Slade had threatened to throw her into that room. Yesterday it dawned on Monica how thin the line between death and survival is in this hell hole.

Vince thumbed through an old issue of *Penthouse* when Monica entered. He glanced up at her and then at the clock on the wall behind him.

"What are you doing here so early?"

"I wanted to check on one of the deaders," Monica lied. "The bite wasn't as deep as it should have been. I need to make sure it reanimated."

"No big deal if it didn't. The deaders we stuck in there the other day will take care of that."

"I know. But I don't want anything to go wrong and piss off the Boss."

"Good idea." Vince could not argue with that logic and went back to reading.

Monica stepped into the warehouse. The deaders in the large pen broke into a frenzy and rushed to the end, trying to get at her. Monica moved closer, a part of her wishing they would bust out and tear her apart, a fitting punishment considering what she and the others had done to them. As Monica drew closer to the cage, she extended her hand, intending to stick her fingers between the links and end this nightmare.

Monica stopped inches from the cage when she spotted the little girl who had been the last turned among Moon's people. The crystal blue eyes had devolved into milky orbs, and decaying skin replaced the once cherubic face. Its teeth chewed at the links, desperate to get at her.

A second deader shoved through the horde until it stood behind the little girl deader. Monica immediately recognized the chewed-off nose and bite marks on its right cheek as belonging to Renee. Their eyes locked. For a moment, Monica thought Renee recognized her. Then it snarled and lunged, the cage being the only thing that kept it from tearing Monica to shreds.

Monica stepped away, her gaze still fixed on Renee and the little girl. She refused to give in and take the easy way out, letting Slade win without a fight. She knew there would be little chance of preventing him from using the suicide deaders. Being involved in that was something Monica would have to live with for the rest of her life.

Somehow, she had to find a way to escape from Vesta and, if possible, find a way to fight Slade.

"I'M GOING TO miss you." Mr. Spritzer wrapped his hands around Alissa's and held it close to his chest. "You're pretty, and you're sweet."

"Aren't I pretty and sweet?" Roni failed to suppress her smile.

"You are, but you're not interested in me. I'm hoping I can change Alissa's mind."

"I appreciate the offer." Alissa squeezed his hands. "But I'm already taken."

"Lucky guy. You know where to find me if he doesn't treat you well."

"It's a deal."

"How about a goodbye hug?"

"I'll do you one better." Alissa leaned down, hugged Mr. Spritzer, then kissed him on the cheek.

The old man smiled. "Now I can die happy."

"Don't say that," Roni chastised him. "You'll be around for a long time."

"Maybe I'll come back and check on you," added Alissa.

"Now there's a reason to stay alive."

Alissa and Roni exited the room. The two women left the house and headed down the driveway to the clinic.

"I'm going to miss you, too," said Roni. "You've been a major help around here. I doubt I'd have been able to perform the operation on Spritzer without you. Not to mention saving the mesa from the horde."

"No problem. Sadly, it's not my first deader rodeo."

"You do this type of stuff that often?"

"Way more than you can imagine." Alissa did not want to think about how many times.

"You and Chris are like action heroes."

"We're out there trying to survive. You're the hero." Alissa paused to glance back at the house. "All those people in there would have been left to starve to death, or worse, if you hadn't saved them."

"Thank you."

When they reached the clinic, Roni broke out into an uncharacteristic smile. "I have a surprise for you."

"What?"

Roni pointed to the circular driveway in front of the clinic. The Challenger sat parked by the main entrance, repaired except for a few dents in the fenders. Chris examined it, attempting to remain calm but failing. Shithead followed him around the vehicle, his tail wagging.

"O'Brien was able to fix it."

Roni nodded. "He's good at his job."

Overhearing the women, O'Brien switched his attention toward them. "It was easy. The front axle was bent, and the alignment was off. It didn't take long."

"Thank you," said Alissa.

"You're welcome. Besides, I couldn't let a classic car like this be sidelined."

"See?" Chris stood and focused on Alissa, his voice sounding as if he had won an argument. "O'Brien understands."

Alissa shook her head. "Boys and their toys."

"It kept you safe during the accident and should keep you safe on the way home."

"I filled the tank, which should be enough to get you to White Sands. In case it isn't..." O'Brien led Alissa and Chris to the back of the Challenger and opened the trunk. "...I gave you a five-gallon can."

"Or we could use it to burn more deaders," joked Chris.

"Not around here, please. We ruined the road leading up to the mesa yesterday. It has ruts all over it from where the asphalt melted and hardened. I used the tractor to push the Ryder aside so you can get by, but pieces of the truck are melted into the ground, so be careful when you leave."

"We will." Chris turned to Alissa. "Ready?"

She nodded.

Chris opened the driver's door. "Come on, boy."

Shithead barked once. He jumped in front, lunged over the console into the back, and spun around facing front.

Chris shook O'Brien's hand. "You did a great job repairing her."

"My pleasure. It was fun. If you want to remove it, I'll take it off your hands."

"Deal." Chris slid into the driver's seat and shut the door. Shithead leaned forward and gave him a face bath.

Roni escorted Alissa to the passenger side. "You fit in well here. If you ever decide to take it easy for a change, I always have room for the three of you."

"Why don't you come back to White Sands with us? They have good medical facilities and can care for Mr. Spritzer and the others."

"Thanks, but I can't accept. No one knows we're here, so no one bothers us. It's peaceful. With Slade coming after White Sands, I'd only be putting my patients in harm's way."

"I understand." Alissa embraced Roni. "Good luck here."

"You're the one who needs the luck. I'll say a prayer for you."

Alissa slid into the passenger's seat. Chris started the Challenger and they drove off, heading down the driveway to the clinic. Alissa glanced in the rearview mirror. Roni and O'Brien stood at the bottom of the stairs, watching them leave. Roni waved goodbye.

Chris had to maneuver slowly down the road leading from the top of the mesa. Not only had the asphalt melted, but the corpses of scores of deaders had slipped into the asphalt and became embedded when it solidified. The same happened at the bottom, only this time including pieces of the truck that fell off during the fire. The charred wreck sat upright and at an angle across the road, allowing just enough space for a single vehicle to get by. Chris did, jolting the car when it ran over a deader melted into the road.

Once clear, they followed the road to Route 550 and took it

south for fifty miles before reaching I-25. Chris raced up the exit ramp and merged onto the highway.

In a few hours, they would be back at White Sands.

A Thank You to My Readers

I've spent the last ten years as a full-time independent writer and have never regretted it. In addition to working for the CIA, it has been one of the most fulfilling things I've done with my life. The best part is having fans who read my books, enjoy them, and crave more. I'm incredibly fortunate and grateful I have such a loyal fanbase. You keep reading, and I'll keep writing.

If you enjoyed *Nurse Alissa vs. the Zombies IX: Calm Before the Storm*, please leave a review on Amazon and Goodreads. Reviews drive the algorithms that get a writer's books more exposure. It doesn't have to be lengthy—just a rating and a sentence or two about why you liked it. Also, please post about the book on your social media and tells friends about it. To be successful, I need your support.

I'm currently writing the next Tatyana novel (which will take place in a haunted asylum). I'm also plotting the third book in *The Chronicles of Paul* saga as well as the last Nurse Alissa novel. After that, I'll begin publishing a brand-new horror series.

Thank you all in advance.

Acknowledgments

I know I say this at the end of every novel, but that's because it's true. The fun part of my job is writing. The difficult part is publishing the books, with editing on the top of my frustration list. It's a complicated process. Thankfully, writers are not alone through it all, and those who help out deserve to be recognized.

Many thanks also go out to my beta readers, Doc Fried and Dungeon Dan Uebel, who have been with me since book one. They point out grammatical/spelling errors and inconsistencies and offer their opinion on whether they like the story. I would be lost without them. This book, like all my others, is a much better read because of them.

Doc Fried also gets kudos for editing the scene when Alissa and Roni operate on Mr. Spritzer. I researched how to perform the operation through a YouTube video; Doc Fried filled in the missing sections and corrected my errors. It proves I'm better at writing about surgery than performing it.

As he does with *The Chronicles of Paul* books, Christian Bentulan designed the cover for *Nurse Alissa vs. the Zombies IX: Calm Before the Storm*. His work perfectly fits the mood of these books. I enjoy collaborating with him.

Finally, as always, a major debt of thanks goes to my family, human and furry. Working from home allows me to set my hours, though it's rare if I work less than ten hours a day. Roxie and the new puppy, Fred, are always with me when I write, though sometimes I spend more time keeping Fred out of trouble than at my computer. At night, when I'm in my study editing and managing social media, my cats Archer and Michonne stand in front of my desktop computer, Michonne because she wants to be petted, and Archer to meow because he ran of treats or because he can see the bottom of his food dish. My family never complains (I think they're glad to get rid of me). I couldn't do this without their love, patience, and support. I love them all.

About the Author

Scott M. Baker was born and raised in Everett, Massachusetts, and spent twenty-three years in northern Virginia working for the Central Intelligence Agency. He has traveled extensively through Europe, Asia, and the Middle East, incorporating many of the locations and cultures in his stories. Scott is now retired and lives outside of Concord, New Hampshire, with his wife, his stepdaughter, and two cats who treat him as their human servant.

Scott is currently writing the *Nurse Alissa vs. the Zombies* and *The Chronicles of Paul* series as well as his Tatyana paranormal saga. Previous works include *Operation Majestic*, his first science fiction novel described as *Raiders of the Lost Ark* meets *Back to the Future* – with aliens; *Frozen World*, his first non-zombie post-apocalypse novel; the *Shattered World* series, his five-book young adult post-apocalypse thriller; *The Vampire Hunters* trilogy, about humans fighting the undead in Washington D.C.; *Yeitso*, his homage to the giant monster movies of the 1950s that he loved watching as a kid; the *Rotter World Saga*, a rerelease of his first zombie trilogy; as well as several zombie-themed novellas and anthologies.

Blog: scottmbakerauthor.blogspot.com
Facebook: facebook.com/groups/397749347486177
MeWe: mewe.com/i/scottmbaker
Twitter: twitter.com/vampire_hunters
Instagram: instagram.com/scottmbakerwriter
YouTube:
youtube.com/channel/UC5AyCVrEAncr2E0N5XoyUdg/featured
Wyrd Realities Homepage: www.wyrdrealities.net

You can also sign up for Scott's newsletter, which will be released on the 1st and 15th of every month. He promises not to share your email with anyone or spam the recipients. The newsletter contains advance notices of upcoming releases/events and short stories from the Alissa, Paul, and Tatyana universes that will not be available to the public. You can sign up by clicking the link below.
Newsletter: mailchi.mp/0b1401f1ddb2/scott-m-baker-writer